The Guys Who Spied For China

Gordon Basichis

Published by
Minstrel's Alley
Los Angeles, CA

ISBN: 0-984105 2-0-4
ISBN-13: 9780984105205
LCCN: 2009933977

Cover design by Casey Basichis

Published by Minstrel's Alley
P.O. Box 492332
Los Angeles, CA 90049

www.minstrelsalley.com

To order additional copies, please contact us.
BookSurge
www.booksurge.com
1-866-308-6235
orders@booksurge.com

For Roy

"...We should thoroughly learn the written and spoken languages of all countries so as to translate Western books and newspapers, in order to know what other countries are doing all around us, and also to train men of ability as diplomats. We should send people to travel to all countries in order to enlarge their points of view and enrich their store of information, to observe the strengths and weaknesses, the rise and fall of other countries; to adopt all the good points of other nations and to avoid the bad points from the start. As a result there will be none of the ships and weapons of any nation, which we shall not be able to make, and none of the machines or implements which we shall not be able to improve."
—-T'an Ssu-T'uang, 1897

chapter

ONE

It was winter in Van Nuys. Winter in Southern California could never evoke the frosty bleakness of the northern states, but on the right night it was still capable of creating an ambience of urban drear and desolation. The streets were empty; traffic was sparse. Gusts of wind blew leaves and trash. I was sitting in the shadows inside Noah Brown's ancient Chevy El Camino, sipping bad coffee from a Styrofoam cup, my eyes cast toward a dumpster-ridden alleyway that divided the tacky shops on Van Nuys Boulevard from the tacky apartments two and three stories above the street.

"That's it." Noah pointed to one ugly apartment building that was nearly indistinguishable from the next. "He lives in the back."

I nodded and studied the dark windows in the second floor rear. A creepy feeling swept over me as I focused on the older, cheaper vehicles parked in the carport on the street level just underneath the building.

"You sure he's not there?" It was less a question and more a plea for reassurance.

Noah gestured. "See the empty space, the last space on the last row? That's where he parks his car."

I nodded, catching the sounds of blue-collar din—a dish clattering in some unknown kitchen, violence from an overloud TV. The smell of a hundred microwave dinners mingled with the garbage odor spiraling from a couple dozen dumpsters. It was bleak and banal, and it stood in sharp contrast to the pre-conceived glamour of cloak-and-dagger romance. But, in fact, it was the banality itself that heightened the danger that lay just a few yards away.

"He may be a contract player, working for Louie's friends. He may be here on his own. It's too early to tell."

I nodded, turning to look at my companion, Noah Brown. Noah was a one of a kind, a government spook with a social and scientific pedigree. Having traveled with Noah for more than a year, I knew all too well about the many times and many places Noah had sat waiting in the darkness, waiting for his prey. Noah's gray hair and angular face were appropriately noirish in the shadows of his faded beige El Camino. Despite his sixty-odd years of age, Noah remained the ever-faithful adventure junkie, seeking his own peculiar gratifications, which he sometimes cloaked in the guise of patriotic ideology. The El Camino, like the older and seemingly fragile Noah, was deceptively virile, filled with spy gear, weapons and a powerhouse engine.

"Either way, I don't want him around causing a ruckus," Noah went on. "The last thing I need is to go chasing him all over the country. Not with all this other business on my plate."

"How did he get into the country?" I asked.

"Slipped in," Noah shrugged matter-of-factly. "Happens all the time. They're in and out of here. Sometimes we catch them, sometimes we don't. But Yomiya, he's one of their big chief muckety mucks. He gets loose and..." Noah let his voice trail off.

I nodded in understanding. I looked to the apartment where Dennis Yomiya was living. Yomiya, native Japanese, was a high-ranking member of the old Red Brigade, and was rumored to be selling his skills to the highest bidder. Surely he was worth his price. Yomiya was a solid professional who reportedly specialized in terrorist bombings and political assassinations. For years he had eluded law enforcement and intelligence agencies, in Europe especially. He was a former college professor who had embraced the radical vision a little too tightly, and now he was stuck with the habit of killing and mayhem. Yomiya was a rogue without legitimacy and without a country to call his own.

"So what do you want me to do?" I asked.

"Find his mailbox," Noah said, handing me a key. "And take whatever mail's inside. It'll help us establish his current network. Remember, he's going under the name Katayama."

"This key will work?" I asked, holding up the key he had given me. "You're sure?"

Noah barely smiled. I knew that miserly smile was all the assurance I was getting.

"And be careful. This guy is a pro. I mean he's marquee material. He spooks easily, and he can put a knife through your eye at twenty yards."

"You have any other words of encouragement?"

"Look around. But don't dawdle up there."

I got out of the car hoping I was ready for the unthinkable and the unexpected. I was frightened. I knew I was no match for a renowned terrorist, and my youthful sense of immortality had, a few precious years before, left for parts unknown. I made my way through the rear walkway and into the spare and modest courtyard where the tenants entered their apartments. There were several doors facing the concrete courtyard, with a stairwell leading to the second floor of apartments. Yellow lamplight from inside the apartments slipped out through the cheap drapes and aluminum frame windows, casting shadows of the withering banana tree on the weathered stucco wall. I found the mailbox marked Katayama, Yomiya's cover name, and slipped the key into the lock. I opened the mailbox just as I heard a car pull up in the driveway.

It was one of those moments frozen in time, when you realize you just committed to a single foolish action that could actually end your life. I stifled the shakes, pulled the single letter out of the mailbox and stuffed it inside my jacket. Reaching into my pocket, I felt for the .25 automatic I had stashed there. It was a cheapo Saturday night special, the kind the anti-gun lobbyists vilify for its predominance in gang marauding and drunken shootouts. If anything, at that particular moment, the .25 was puny and inadequate, more of an ornament than decent protection. I remembered how old gun nuts I knew used to joke that shooting someone with a .25 caliber would only piss him off. I hoped I wouldn't have to disprove that theory.

Yomiya appeared in the mouth of the courtyard, blocking my exit. He was momentarily startled by my presence, but since I made no move toward him, he feigned indifference, barely looking up as I started past him on my way out of the courtyard. He was wearing wire rim glasses, a short leather jacket and his trademark woolen newsboy's cap. At first glance he wasn't threatening at all, more like the college professor of old, lost in his thoughts. But looking closer, there was no denying his wary movement and the deadly aura he projected from deep within.

Either my sixth sense was in tune that night, or I actually did hear his rubber sole sliding every so slightly on the courtyard's surface grit. I turned suddenly, drawing my gun, and found him facing me, his hand reaching inside his jacket pocket. Before I dared think about it, I fired twice. The first bullet caught him flush in the cheekbone, just under the eye, and the other skimmed the side of his face.

Instinctively, he grabbed at his face, grumbling what I was sure was "Shit," in English, before muttering and cursing in what sounded like Japanese. He staggered like a drunk. Sheer fear compelled me to step in to point blank range and fire three times in rapid succession, putting small, bloody holes in his temple. It was like a dream. Echoes and flashes in the tiny courtyard. He was gasping for breath, still weaving and muttering. The blood pooled in his ear and ran down his neck. He dropped hard to his knees, like his feet had been chopped out from under him. I nearly shit when his nine-millimeter pistol spilled out of his jacket and clattered on the concrete. Yomiya muttered something again, in a softer, barely audible tone and then pitched forward on his face. I shot him one more time through the back of his head.

As I walked quickly toward the car, I thought my heart would leap out of my chest. My knees were locked and buckling; my legs were rubber. Somehow I found the presence of mind to stash the hot and smoking pistol into my jacket. It felt warm against my ribs. When I reached the end of the driveway, I found

Noah hobbling toward me on his semi-crippled legs. From the look on his face, he had been afraid for me, and now the creased and worried brow was showing visible signs of relief that I was the one still walking.

"Better get the fuck out of here," I uttered through clenched teeth.

He nodded and started back to the car, moving remarkably fast for a guy with legs the width of cue sticks. As I climbed inside, Noah pulled away slowly. He turned up Van Nuys Boulevard at traffic speed, and a few blocks later he entered the freeway. Moving north on the 101, Noah picked up speed, maneuvering discretely in and out of lanes, checking to see if we were being followed.

"No one on our tail," he said with a fair degree of relief and satisfaction.

I didn't respond.

"You were only supposed to get the mail," he admonished. The fear and concern were still in his voice. It was his way of covering up for sticking me in a dangerous situation.

"Well, what the hell," I gritted. "There was a sudden change in plans."

"I know," he relented. "Is he dead?"

I stared. "I sure fucking hope so."

"You did good then," Noah acknowledged, lighting up a cigarette. Just what I needed at that moment, second hand smoke.

I sat in silence while Noah covered miles on the freeways, making sure we weren't being followed. When he was satisfied we were safe, he drove to his house, where Noah, the scientist, prepared a glass vat of highly concentrated sulfuric acid and tossed in the gun. We watched in meditative silence while the

.25 caliber pistol dissolved like an Alka Seltzer, providing us both with a bit of relief. Dissolve the evidence. Clearly, Noah was used to the drill.

I had a lot on my mind. I had just killed somebody, and I realized it wasn't enough to rationalize he intended to kill me. I was so scared, I acted first, and by acting first I got lucky. In the flash of understanding I realized two significant precepts. The first was fear could be the overwhelming guiding force in a time of crisis, and it could produce better results than professional skills. The second was that, to my good fortune, when people hear gunshots, they do not run outside to see what's going on.

In my head I replayed my shooting of Yomiya, my watching him die awkwardly and ugly, like a puppet cut suddenly from its strings. Killing him was not an act to be taken lightly, and any show of nonchalance would be pure bravado, denying the feelings I grappled with inside. Killing was wrong for the usual reasons. I knew that. A momentary wave of nausea overcame me as I wrestled my conscience. I recognized Yomiya was the terrorist sonofabitch responsible for the murders of a number of innocent people and that the planet wouldn't be missing him. I glanced at Noah; he was already whispering to someone on the telephone, making sure Yomiya's body vanished without a trace, like some dead alley cat swept up by the animal regulations people and dumped in an unmarked grave.

I soon dispelled the nausea, and I found the struggle with my conscience was inexplicably transplanted by a life confirming rush. I had faced death and I had survived. I wondered if I would ever be forced to kill again. And could I ever get so used to killing that my conscience no longer affected me? Like Noah. I sensed in the darker, more manipulative recesses of Noah's brain, he certainly hoped I'd become more like him. I looked over to where he was sitting, puffing on his cigarette, working out our next set of moves. I watched the last bits of gunmetal dissolve in the acid. And in the silence of the canyons, punctuated briefly by howling coyotes and the occasional rustle of sage, I wondered how in the hell I had ended up here.

chapter

TWO

For me, this story began in the dentist's chair in the autumn of 1982. That's when I first met Dr. Louis Dubin. He had been recommended to me as an excellent dentist. Dubin was a garrulous man with an affable personality punctuated by the distinctive adenoidal register of the Mid-Atlantic States. He was in his late fifties and looked like your basic aging hip booster who had outgrown his excesses and settled down. He had wavy gray hair and the ash white beard of an upscale bohemian. He wore wire-rimmed glasses and corduroy Levi's with button down oxford shirts. Behind the glasses, his steel-blue eyes were filled with scrutiny and just a hint of menace. When we shook hands, he exhibited the powerful grip acquired by most dentists after years of pulling teeth and digging out cavities.

Unlike most physicians, who try to maintain a cool and objective professional distance, Louis preferred being chummy and chatty. He was a good listener, and he liked to talk about himself, qualities that made him skillful in jumping from the introductory phase of our relationship to easy familiarity in less than an hour.

"Nina tells me you're a writer," he offered, referring to the woman who had recommended him. "A lot of writers are patients of mine. I get a lot of Hollywood people."

He told me how he relished being the dentist to show business personalities who worked both in front of and behind the camera. In a city of contacts, where hair stylists and restaurateurs are sometimes as responsible for initial deal making as attorneys and agents, his patients offered a modest amount of networking currency. His practice provided him with a decent income, which he used to maintain his comfortable bachelor's lifestyle and an upper six-figure house in the Santa Monica Mountain range overlooking Beverly Hills.

Dr. Dubin was probably the first dentist since the infamous Doc Holliday to keep a gun holstered within short reach of his dental tools. It was a strange vision, this Colt .45 semiautomatic pistol resting a few feet from where Louis prepared his steel amalgam fillings and mixed his dental cement.

"Why the gun?" I asked. "The ultimate anesthetic?"

"I have a permit to carry," he boasted. "Which is almost impossible to get these days, with all these liberals wanting to grab our weapons."

"If you don't want them taking your guns, then don't leave them out where they can see them."

"Doesn't do any good in a drawer. If trouble comes, you have only seconds to defend yourself. You have to keep the gun close by."

"Doesn't it frighten patients?"

"It didn't frighten you."

"I'm not your average patient."

Louis smiled, knowingly. "I sensed that," he said. "I've always been good at sensing these things."

Instead of the usual cotton-stuffed, saliva-filled innocuous mutterings between dentist and patient, Dubin sang the anthem of the Second Amendment.

"I told myself a long time ago, I don't intend to be the victim," Louis insisted. "No place is safe, really."

"Yeah, Louie, maybe you do have a point," I conceded.

"Louis!" he corrected immediately, his body stiffening. I had tripped over his one concession to formality.

"Louis," I repeated. "Sorry about that."

He nodded to signify it was a forgivable transgression.

"I keep a gun in every room in the house," Louis confided as he picked at my teeth with the tools of his trade. "But I carry a Colt .45," he said, pointing to the semi-automatic as his weapon of choice.

I nodded, smiling.

"What's the smile?" Louis demanded.

I shrugged. "Nothing."

"Look, I believe you take care of your own. Because if you don't, then who's going to do it for you? The government?

"My friends and I, we take care of each other. Some guys I know are in their forties and fifties, and they can still rappel cliffs as good as any SAS commando."

"It's always good to have friends."

"Especially my friends. Maybe you would like to come up and meet them? I have these get-togethers every month or so. I order in food, and we sit and talk. Gun people, mostly. Some are professionals, like me, and some are technology guys. Others are the real thing—ex-law enforcement, government types. Spooks. A few ex-military. A couple of active mercenaries. Once in awhile some Hollywood people show up. It's an interesting group."

"I'll bet it is."

"Good," he smiled, affectionately slapping my arm. "I'll give you directions."

Most people, especially my friends who were politically correct and possessed of at least a rudimentary social consciousness, would have bowed out politely and then scrambled in search of another dentist. But not me. I was the street-smart schmuck who was determined to follow this new discovery wherever it led him. Why is that? On one hand, I don't know, really. On the other hand, there are probably a dozen reasons, some of them deeply rooted psychologically and the rest a mixture of story seeking and just being crazy.

I always had a flirtation with danger and the shadowy creatures that thrived in dangerous worlds. For some reason I was never fearful of that world. I was no angel myself, but nothing I ever had done compared with some of the fearsome creatures I had met on that toll road of life. I was basically a nice guy who over the years had formed acquaintances with the wise guys and tough guys I had met either as a journalist or through fate and circumstance.

I was also a published novelist who enjoyed modest success writing for television and film. I was looking for a story, but more than a story, perhaps. I was restless and looking for a new lease on life. A recent flurry of abrupt but significant downturns, including the violent death of a friend, was forcing me to reassess my current direction. If I had any direction to even reassess.

I went to Louis Dubin's party out of curiosity. I went because fate had pointed me that way. Intuition dictated that in this unlikely direction lay my destiny. I was stepping through the looking glass, and my life, my world and everything about it, would soon be turned around.

chapter

THREE

Louis' two story house occupied a flag lot in the Santa
Monica Mountain Range, overlooking several fabled canyons and
the city skyline, which shimmered in the distance a thousand
feet below. He lived in a modest sized house with a million dollar view. On a clear winter day you could see the Pacific Ocean
to the west, while a snowcapped Mt. Wilson towered in the east.
The house itself was hidden away, so without detailed directions
it would have been easy for me to miss it. On a dark night the
narrow driveway was lost among the overhanging shrubbery and
the two adjacent properties.

I announced myself on the intercom, and when the electric
gate swung open, I passed through.

Louis was waiting for me in the foyer. "Glad you could make it," smiled Louis, approaching, tossing his arms for a warm, friendly hug. "I wasn't sure you would."

There were twenty-five to thirty people seated about the living room, or talking around the dining room table that had been extended for the occasion. A couple of faces I recognized quickly. Hollywood people.

"What would you like to drink?" Louis asked. "I have wine or beer, soda and Perrier."

"A beer would be nice," I told him, and he led me into the narrow, but well ordered galley kitchen, accented by a pot rack and houseplants.

As he fished in the fridge for a beer for me, he gestured to the upper cabinets. "If you want a glass, they're up in there."

I opened the cabinet and was greeted by a neat assortment of sparkling glasses and an older police issue .38-caliber revolver wedged between the dessert plates and coffee mugs. I removed a glass from the shelf and watched in silence as Louis poured my beer.

He smiled again and led me back into the living room. "Let me introduce you around."

I shook hands as Louis made a valiant attempt to introduce me to his guests. They were mostly Average Joe's, dressed in Levi's and L.L. Bean. They were so ordinary; in fact, they seemed out of place in the more glitzy environs of Beverly Hills. It was their Average Joe looks that made them more dangerous. These weren't the archetypical guys Hollywood had taught us to fear, no cinematic heavies in leather and sneers. These were almost the kind of guys you found at model railroad fetes or memorabilia conventions. What passion they aroused inside their plaid shrouded frames was stimulated not primarily by the usual vices, but by their affection for weapons.

They talked the finer points of caliber size and grain loads, discussing magazine capacity at length. They spoke of bullet velocity, explosive force and penetration. They compared and contrasted the destructive merits of hollow point ammo with the reliability of full metal casings. They mentioned windage and elevation, necessary calculations related to shooting from a distance. In their zeal, they reminded me of the Camel-smoking motor heads I knew growing up, who squatted on milk crates, trading arcane facts about transmissions and engine blocks into the wee hours of the morning. For me, it was another case of post-modern overload.

Still, I was intrigued by the camaraderie among this folksy group, who in their social isolation were brought together by Louis. Most were polite and easygoing, throwbacks to an older school of manners and circumspection. And not all were geeks. A few of them were clearly dangerous men, powerfully built, former mercenaries with eyes still scanning the third world shit holes that were permanently etched in the back of their minds. A few had served in law enforcement, and several more were from that murky background where you didn't ask questions. The rest were technocrats or engineers, either self-employed or working for major corporations. Some were veterans of military service, and some were just professional people who were in love with their guns.

As I talked to them, I found most were devout libertarians who hadn't much use for the government. They fell into what I considered the no man's land between left wing and right wing, and they embraced a somewhat confusing agenda of civil rights and free form capitalism, coupled with a distrust of bureaucracies and multi-national corporations. They were strong as a unit, and they were smart enough to know their power was in numbers.

They made no excuses for their weapons lust or the consequential social rejection it caused them. At best, they were only vaguely aware they stood in marked contrast to media driven society. It didn't seem to faze them that they were neither politically correct nor topically fashionable. They didn't wish to be outsiders, really. In fact, if given their preference, they all wanted a larger slice of the American Pie. Instead of the pie they had each other.

Louis served as the Den Mother to the gang; he was the provider of sanctuary. Clearly, they adored him.

"What do you think of my friends?" he asked, pointing to a few, including Tom Raymond, a bearded middle-aged man in a wheelchair, who Louis proclaimed to be a former Navy fighter pilot. Raymond's wife, Linda, was standing behind her husband, arguing the fine points of political something with Nelson Stackhouse, a man I had met earlier.

"Quite a collection,"

Louis smiled. "I trust these guys with my life. And they trust me with theirs. "Here," he said, gesturing toward a short man in spectacles with nervous eyes and wavy hair who had just come over to join us. "I'd like you to meet a very special friend of mine. Ray Dannenberg."

"Louis told me a lot about you," Ray smiled, extending his hand.

"I hope he hasn't said too much."

"Louis likes to talk a lot," Ray laughed, and Louis laughed in complicity. "He said you're a writer with anti-government leanings."

"I wouldn't go that far. I'm just a guy with reasonable sense of history."

"You couldn't possibly be pro-government," he insisted. "Not how they treat us today. Every time you look around it's always mucking around in our business."

"And what business is that, Ray?"

"Ray manufactures electronics components for the cable and telecommunications industries. Louis glanced at Ray to see if he described his business correctly.

"Seems basic enough. Why is the government on your case?"

"They're all over me, about everything. With all their rules and regulations. To say nothing of the IRS."

"Sounds like you should start a revolution or find a better accountant."

"I'm up for the revolution. What about you?"

I shrugged. "I have a terrific accountant."

Ray took his time in appraising my answer. He laughed finally. "Louis is right. You're an okay guy."

"He's a friend now," Louis chimed in, turning to me for greater emphasis. "Anyone does wrong to a friend, then he does wrong to us."

"Tough talk for a dentist."

Louis smiled, and it was a colder smile than I was used to. "I'm a dentist with a gun. That makes all the difference."

Not long after, I took particular note of a sober looking man sitting patiently in the corner. Unlike the others, this man was dressed conservatively in a gray suit and tie. His graying hair was swept back from a lined but handsome face. He leaned forward in his chair, quietly observing the chitchat. He looked like a cop, the serious kind, a lifelong professional who had miraculously avoided the burnout. But he wasn't a cop. Louis told me that much and more.

"He's my neighbor," Louis whispered. "He is very high up in the federal government."

When I looked doubtful, Louis persisted.

"It's true. I've seen limousines come in the middle of the night and whisk him off to God knows where. I'm telling you, he's a very powerful guy. It's scary."

I found it fascinating that of all the commando types, the shooters and soldiers of fortune, the one guy Louis most feared was the elderly gentleman sitting alone in the corner.

"What's he doing here then?"

"Like I said, he's my neighbor."

"But nobody talks to him, really."

I glanced over to the corner where the gray-headed man in the silver gray suit was staring back at me. He knew we were talking about him. His eyes were intense and piercing, yet somewhat inviting. He nodded to me, and I nodded back.

"Come on," said Louis. "I'll introduce you."

Moments later I met Noah Brown.

"And just what are you doing here?" he asked as we shook hands. It was more of a challenge than a question.

"It's life as an art form," I told him.

He smiled, not entirely sure what I was driving at. "Not high art, certainly," he said after a pause.

I smiled.

"C'mon, sit down a minute," he offered, indicating the space beside him.

"Sorry. I have to get going."

Noah was by disturbed by what he deemed my sudden departure.

"Was it something that I said?" he asked.

"No. But what's waiting for me is prettier than you."

He grunted reluctant approval. "Can't fault you for that. She have a girlfriend?"

"Just two cats and a litter box."

"No thanks," he replied in mock disgust.

I left soon after, closing the door to one of life's chapters and opening another. Destiny had just intervened and dropped kicked my ass in a whole new direction.

chapter

FOUR

Two weeks later, and much to my surprise, Noah Brown was on the phone to me. He wanted to take me to dinner. I considered making jokes about me not being the type who fucked on the first date, but I sensed this was hardly Noah's brand of humor.

"Meet me at Adriano's?"

Adriano's was an upscale Italian restaurant in the Beverly Glen Centre, a strip mall at the crest of the Santa Monica Mountain range, just below Mulholland Drive. The Glen Centre was far more unique than the majority of strip centers in America. Instead of the usual suburbanite consumer traffic, the Glen Centre serviced a tonier, show business crowd who could shop and eat in relative privacy within a few minutes' drive of their homes. The Glen Centre parking lot looked more like a dealership for luxury European automobiles than a parking lot for a mini-mall. On any given day the crowded asphalt boasted Mercedes and BMW's of every conceivable model, Jaguars, Porsches, Ferraris, and a Rolls Royce or Bentley for that extra measure of extravagance. If you drove up in a junker, then you were probably just working there.

When I arrived, Noah Brown was waiting for me at his table. As I approached, I watched the waiter fawn over Brown like he was a familiar and valued patron. Brown was sipping wine and picking at the Italian bread in a leisurely manner, demanding softer butter. It appeared as if he had been there awhile, waiting alone, despite the fact that every table was taken and anxious dinner patrons were crowded into the bar.

"How are you?" Brown asked me, rising out of his chair to shake my hand. I felt his eyes assessing my jacket and slacks; relieved I knew how to dress for formal restaurants. "Have you eaten here before?"

"A few times."

He nodded. Even in the atmospheric restaurant lighting, I noticed Brown's crippled physique. His handsome face was mounted on the body of a troll. He was hunchbacked, and when he stood up to greet me, his suit pants were hiked up, and I noticed his legs were withered so badly they weren't much thicker than the average pair of arms.

He smiled faintly and looked around. "What's really nice about this place are all the beautiful women. You like women?"

I nodded. It was an obvious and leading question.

"I used to date my fair share of actresses," he said, perhaps as his way of assuring me of his sexual preferences, given the invitation to dinner. He named a few brand name actresses from the fifties and sixties, and if his boasting was true, then I was impressed.

"If nothing else, they kept me entertained and open minded. But they got older and went onto other things."

"And you? You didn't grow older?"

He smiled. "I'd like to think not. Up here," he said, indicating his mind, "I'm still in my prime. Everywhere else..." he let his voice trail off.

"Still chasing romance. Only you are finding it tougher to catch."

"Something like that. I guess I like lighting candles for the way things used to be."

The waiter arrived and gushed about specials. Noah ordered like he was commanding forces, giving the waiter special instructions about his veal chop and the consistency of his pasta. He ordered a bottle of expensive Cabernet Sauvignon and made a pretense of judging its flavor before it was poured.

"I have a piece of a winery up in Napa Valley," he said. "We produce some world class wine up there. Including this," he said, tapping the wine bottle's label.

"Louis did say you were a man of many interests."

"Sooner or later I'll end up in a wheelchair. So I try to keep as active as possible, while I still can."

He told me he was a former fighter pilot and an intrepid cold warrior; he had been shot and stabbed, bombed and poisoned. That was but part of the freight he paid for frequent trips under and over the Iron Curtain and for skulking about in strange and forbidden frontiers. I could see as he boasted about the dozens of wounds on his body, there were immeasurable scars on his soul.

"Believe it or not, in high school I was a six foot, two hundred pound line backer. Before a spent twenty millimeter cannon shell from a Jap Zero busted up my back and chest.

"An accident at the Skunk Works took care of my legs. Hydrogen gas explosion killed men eighty, ninety feet away. I went up on a forty-five degree angle and hit my head on a pole. I survived, only because I was at the epicenter of the explosion. Still, I had broken fourteen ribs and both collarbones. My thyroid still gives me trouble, possibly because of the double dose of tetanus shots I received for the puncture wounds and abrasions. I'm lucky to be alive."

"We're all lucky to be alive," I offered, sipping on my wine. Glancing around, I saw the rich and famous, the Hollywood powerhouses and the mighty corporate Angelenos. I wondered what secret source of power was sitting across from me, this almost mythical creature in a broken down shell. I marveled at the fact he was living his mystery life out in plain sight. I felt his eyes on me, seeking, probing, and learning about me from my every gesture. I felt like I was being studied by an alien being.

Noah allowed us time to finish our dinner, before he tried another approach. "What has Louie told you about me?"

"He said you had a lot of juice in the federal government, and that you're no one to be fucked with."

"Louie has a big mouth," he said, lighting up a cigarette. "You don't mind if I smoke."

It wasn't a question.

"Yeah, Louie does have a big mouth. But if you are all the stuff that Louis claims, then why would you tell him? And why do you call him Louie, when he prefers to be called Louis?"

"Because it gets on his nerves."

"He's scared to death of you. I'm sure you know that."

"I prefer it that way. You know why?"

I shook my head. I could only imagine.

Noah studied his cigarette ash as if in the glowing embers there lay the secret to life. "The day he moved in, they unloaded a truckload of weapons and stored them in his house."

"A truckload?" I asked skeptically. "That's impressive."

Noah nodded and started clicking them off. "A truckload. M-16's, AR-15's. Military issue. Civilian issue. Some of them were fully automatic. I went over to do my good neighbor routine, and I'm watching his mover buddies stacking them up in his bedroom, along with the ammo to go with them. Later he had these big, custom built walk-in safes installed under the stairwell, just to hold all this crap. Supposedly the safes are booby trapped, but I really don't know."

Noah paused to gauge my reaction. When he was satisfied he was making the intended impression, he went on.

"I tell him his house has a lovely view, and you know what he tells me? He says his house is in an absolutely defensible position."

"Maybe it's a new twist on neighborhood watch."

Noah held up his hand, a sign for me to wait before passing judgment. "Then he finds out I may know a thing or two, so he starts pumping me for information about burglar alarms, security gates, defensive landscaping."

"Houses are robbed all the time up here. I have met some of the people who rob them."

Noah shook his head in frustration. I wasn't getting it. "Louie wasn't stopping at a burglar alarm. He told me he wanted to build a mutual defense perimeter around our houses."

"I see your point. Most neighbors settle for a cinderblock wall."

Noah shook his head in frustration. No, I didn't even begin to see his point. "I used to see him walking around, making penetration runs on his property."

"Excuse me?"

"He's crazy, you know. You do realize that? I could have him sent to prison."

"He could practice his dentistry in there. A lot of inmates would be grateful."

Brown demurred, considered, and then began very slowly. "There are some branches of the government in which it's a federal crime to identify an agent. The crime is punishable by stiff fines and jail time. Did you know that?"

"It's never come up before. But if I had to guess, judging by what both Louis and you had to say, is the National Reconnaissance Office one of them?"

Brown allowed me the satisfaction of a half-smile. "The National Reconnaissance Office doesn't exist," he proclaimed. "But if it did exist, yes, identifying any of its operatives would be punishable by stiff fines and a prison sentence."

"So where does that leave you?"

"A lot of places and nowhere. You can look me up, but you'll never find me. I go all the way back to the OSS. In the office of Dr. Vannevar Bush, who was the head of science and research. I've chaired or co-chaired several Presidential commissions, and I was adviser to eleven presidential administrations during my tenure."

"Well, that's where we're different. The only president I ever knew was the head of my high school fraternity. And I thought he was kind of a pussy."

He smiled. "I was part of the development team in the missile and space programs.

"I was a classic underachiever. And not much of a team player. But no matter; I thought you weren't supposed be telling me this stuff."

He shrugged it off. "I'm retired now. I'm worth a few bucks," he allowed in classic understatement. "I hold over seventy patents, mostly in radio and electronics. My monuments for after I'm gone."

I smiled, wondering if he really believed that in this world of sound bite memories, anyone would remember the inventor of esoteric devices.

"So what are you doing up at Louie's?" he asked, stirring the sugar in his coffee.

I shrugged. "Don't know, really. It's fascinating in a surreal kind of way. But more importantly, what are you doing there? Somehow I doubt if it's languishing in your retirement."

Noah just smiled enigmatically. "I know I shouldn't, but I'm really in the mood for dessert."

chapter

FIVE

A week after my dinner with Noah Brown, Louis called and asked me to come to his house. He was excited, which caused him to speak in the clipped, staccato cadence of an Army Drill Instructor from a bad war movie. It was one of several personas I had watched Louis assume from time to time. On occasion I had been in his company when a change in stimuli resulted in conspicuous character shifts, like someone was changing channels. But while channel surfing was a deliberate action, Louis' personality shifts were involuntary, a reflex response to his social environment, much like an octopus who alters color and shape to accommodate its surroundings.

Every so often I'd hit him with buzzwords, just to see how he'd respond. It was like giving a word association test in an aberrant dimension. Like the octopus, Louis' character took on the color of the subject matter, switching from Louis the professional nice guy to Louis the skulking legionnaire. In one instant he could be warm and playful, and in the next he could be curt with foreboding emanations rising from a darker, deeper place. He could also be the studious professor, the near-academic willing to teach and eager to learn. Especially spooky were the sudden bouts of silence when I'd observe his almost total withdrawal. He would brood several moments and then return, usually switching back to his nice guy motif. He wanted to be loved again.

When I reached Louis' house, he was all smiles and hospitality, the clipped, rigid cadence gone from his voice. Two wine case sized wooden crates of NATO issue 7.62mm rifle cartridges were stacked on his living room carpet.

"Nice accent pieces. From Crate and Barrel?"

"For the Galils," he answered offhandedly, referring to the Israeli assault rifle. He sounded as if the bullets were plant food for a new bed of roses.

He offered me a beer. Sitting at his dining room table, I noticed a spotting scope was pointed out the window overlooking the canyons.

"Spying on your neighbors?" I joked, nodding toward the spotting scope.

"It helps me keep a watch on things."

"I'll bet it does."

He didn't get it. I was being light, and he was being cataclysmic. Louis peered through the spotting scope. With a grandiose sweep of his arm, he gestured to the canyons and the city below.

"You never know when trouble comes. With the tactical advantage this position gives us, we could defend this house indefinitely, if we had to. We could pick off intruders without any problem."

"We?" I asked, hoping I was not being included in his mythic last stand.

He looked puzzled; silly question. "My friends."

"What makes you think we're facing that kind of catastrophe? You're talking total breakdown of civil order. Aren't you?"

"I'm prepared for anything," he declared emphatically.

I nodded, thinking, here we are, grown men sipping imported beer and speculating on Armageddon in a city where the maid quitting or a bad parking space was regarded as a major calamity.

"Noah said he had dinner with you," he began.

"Yeah. He called me out of the blue."

Louis smiled. "He likes you. Noah doesn't like too many people."

"I'm sure not too many people are overjoyed about Noah."

Louis scratched his ear and took off his glasses, examining them for smudges as he summoned his thoughts. He began what I took for his sales pitch.

"Noah's a valuable guy. If you can get close to him, that would be terrific. Noah can help make us a pile of money. You like money, don't you?"

"Noah's a government spook. It's like playing with fire."

"Everything worth having involves a little risk."

"Louis," I reminded him. "There are situations where the consequences outweigh the potential rewards. You told me yourself, you're afraid of Noah Brown."

Louis sighed and tried to relax. He let a moment pass before he started in again. "Noah is on the cutting edge of government related technology. Radio frequency, imaging systems and microwave technology. That kind of expertise is worth a fortune on the open market. Just what he could do for Ray Dannenberg's business alone could be worth millions."

"The guy only asked me to dinner," I said with more than a little edge to my voice. "He doesn't want to marry me. So why credit me with so much influence?"

"Because you're a natural at it. I may be just a dentist, but I'm also a smart judge of talent. And your true talent is in working people. It was obvious from the first day I saw you. You're the natural go-between. Look, if anyone can talk Noah's language, it's you."

"Noah's language is science. I got "C's" in Science."

"Take your time. Think it over. You'll see what I mean."

Louis was smiling now, believing he had made his point. He had, in a sense. For the first time, I realized Louis had carved a niche for me in this gun loving social club. To him I was the polished one, a potential liaison between his disaffected coterie and the mainstream forces of media and industry. I felt like a ball that had been put into play.

I was just getting ready to say goodbye when Louis stood up and gestured for me to follow.

"I've been meaning to give you fresh herbs from my garden."

When we were outside in his yard, Louis fished out a trowel and quart-sized Zip Loc plastic bags and squatted in the dirt. Digging among the neat and tidy rows of vegetables and herbs, he spoke to me as if the conversation inside the house had never happened. We were friends again, just talking organic herbs.

"Nothing better than fresh Basil," he said. "A little mint, some nice fresh Rosemary. Smell," he commanded, putting the open bag under my nose.

He handed me three Zip Loc bags, and he was going for a fourth. I wasn't sure if he was the kid playing happily in the sandbox, or the guilty friend trying to make amends for forcing Noah Brown upon me.

"Louis, that's enough already. I've got enough Basil here for twenty years."

"Oh." He shrugged, struggling with the idea that I had rejected his generosity.

"Let me get you a couple of eggplants then," he offered with newfound enthusiasm.

While he dug around for eggplants, I meandered toward his open garage, gazing in awe at the fifty-gallon containers of water and the cache of survival foods stocked up on floor-to-ceiling shelves. No doubt, this man was prepared for disaster of Biblical proportions. With the food he had stored, he would have to live to a hundred to consume it all. I soon realized the stockpile wasn't only for him, but was part of that obscure "us" and "they" scenario about which he had been intimating since I first met him.

"That's nothing," he said, coming up beside me to admire his cache. He waved me inside the garage. "I've got plenty more buried in the ground."

"Say what?" I had heard it before, but now, after sessions with Noah, I wanted to hear it again.

"I've got all kinds of ammo and supplies stored under my lawn," he said, as if it were the most natural thing in the world.

"This takes some major faith in Armageddon," I remarked.

Louis laughed. It struck him funny. So funny, in fact, he was still chortling when he reached behind several boxes on his shelf and plucked from a smaller box a glass ounce bottle of clear liquid. We were off on another show and tell.

"See this?" he asked, shaking the liquid, which filled a little more than half the bottle. "Ricin. A couple drops of this stuff will kill an elephant. Just think what happens when you dump it into a water supply."

"A lot of dead elephants."

Louis frowned in confusion, the bottle of Ricin still in his hand. I could see he was troubled by the disapproving look on my face.

"Why would you ever want to poison the water supply?"

"You just never know," he shrugged.

I knew. "I don't even piss upstream, because I wouldn't want someone to drink it."

I suddenly felt like had fallen into the rabbit hole, and the Mad Hatter was serving Ricin instead of tea, and the White Rabbit was storing time bombs under the lawn. To cap off the perfect unsettling moment, I noticed fifty-pound bags of ready-mix cement, standing like dusty midgets in the far corner of the garage.

"You building another patio?"

He shook his head. "For weighing down bodies. I personally had four people executed," he admitted, giving it time to sink in.

"When?"

"A long time ago. But I keep them around for my friends to use. You've met some of my friends. Anything happens, and they come in a van, sweep up the bodies and dump them far out at sea.

No one ever finds them. No one ever knows. If you ever need our services, I'm happy to help you. I've got plenty of body bags."

He said it like he was offering to roll new sod. I glanced over to the cement bags and noticed a dusty ring on the plywood pallet, the tell tale sign that one of the bags had been recently removed. I felt my bowels churn and the hairs and sweat prick the back of my neck. I had been around other dangerous and violent men, but Louis was the kind of psychopath that could murder on a whim. I didn't really fear him, actually, but I felt uneasy in the presence of someone who resided in a parallel universe.

I looked again at the dusty ring where a cement bag had once sat like a benched linebacker waiting to be put in the game. I wondered how many other bags were missing; their contents sprinkled dry in body bags, absorbing water on their way to the bottom of the sea. Quite a few must have already been assigned to sea duty, since Louis always bought things in discount quantity. I caught Louis out of the corner of my eye staring at the bags of cement with what undoubtedly seemed like a touch of nostalgia.

Noah was right. Louis was crazy. The paranoid schizophrenic had just played me a medley of his greatest hits. It was time to make myself scarce.

chapter

SIX

Since our first dinner, Noah Brown and I had been meeting on what was more or less a regular basis. About once or twice a week we had lunch or dinner, usually in the Glen Centre on the top of Mulholland Drive. There were occasions when Noah left town for extended periods, giving short notice and no clue where he was going. Upon his return he would call, inviting me out, and again we would lunch among the celebrities and trophy wives in the Beverly Glen Centre. For the most part, Noah insisted he pick up the check from his perpetual wad of hundred dollar bills.

In spite of our little masquerade, we were forming a closer friendship. I was now picking him up at his house, where he lived with Laurie, his housekeeper. She was a charming woman in her early sixties. She held remnants of the backwater countenance of someone who grew up in LA when it was still a mess of rustic towns searching for a freeway. The house itself was stylish enough, a mid-century ranch type, but the exterior belonged in the far reaches of industrial LA.

Metal of every description was piled in stacks or heaped about the walled-in yard. There were stacks of long copper tubing, steel beams and old machinery. An ancient cement mixer stood frozen in time. Along the side of the house, three steel radio towers shot from cement foundations more than sixty feet in the air, looking like the vintage logo of RKO Studios. A half a dozen vehicles occupied the driveway, and an early model satellite dish, halved and rusted, was abandoned in the empty swimming pool.

"My house is a confidential government laboratory," Noah informed me with all solemnity the first time I came over to pick him up. "Until I finish the add-on, I can't have you inside."

"No wonder it's confidential," I told him. "Most people would be embarrassed to live like this. It's like House and Garden had sex with a junkyard, and this is their bastard child. It's a good thing you have the neighbors intimidated."

He furrowed his brow, trying in vain to comprehend the imposition he caused to the neighborhood. Clearly, this was his natural habitat, and he was in his element hobbling around the scrap piles.

"What do you mean? No one's ever complained."

"Because you scare the shit out of them. This is a million dollar-plus neighborhood. They complain if leaves blow across their lawns, yet alone a mess like this."

He shrugged it off like it was the last thing on his mind. It was.

"There's something I want you to do. Louie is going to invite you to a big party to celebrate his nephew's graduation from medical school. I want you to go and see what it's about."

"I think I've had enough of Louie for awhile. Psychopaths can be entertaining, but then they start to wear thin."

Noah learned across the table, conveying urgency. "I'd consider this a special favor."

Dutifully, the night of the party I arrived late at Louis' house and found the kind of Warholian social blending that could be construed as a twisted art form. Two thirds of the guests were Peter's medical student friends and associates, while the other third consisted of Louis' extended family of techno-happy gun nuts. In what I saw as their reluctant homage to their painful days as high school misfits, Louis' friends huddled among themselves, eyeballing the pretty young women who were ignoring them. I noticed most of the gun boys were drinking more than usual. I couldn't tell if it was because of the heightened festivity or a desperate retreat to the solace that only inebriation could offer.

Ray Dannenberg offered no real answers when he cornered me in the living room. However, he did reveal in his inimitable way that I had been square dancing with a circle of galactic strangers.. It was a drunk and melancholy Dannenberg, who, in lamenting his present life, longed for the good old days when times were simpler and all he had to do was kill people to make a living.

"I put myself through school that way. Assassination."

"Yeah? Me, I worked in a drugstore."

Dannenberg snorted scotch and laughter, and noted with pride how he had saved enough money to start his own business.

"But it's different now," he lamented, staring into his scotch as if he was searching for answers. "It used to be so simple. So easy. Now every time I turn around, I have labor troubles and money issues, one lawsuit after another.

"The responsibility has changed me," he offered in a drunken appraisal of his present woes. "All the worry. It wears your nerves out. I've put on so much weight because of stress."

"You didn't worry then? About getting caught and going to jail?"

"Naw, naw," he shook his head. "Who would be looking for someone like me? A kid. I was so young. One weekend I killed two Germans up at Big Bear and walked out from the crowd without a hitch."

"Ruined their vacation, I'll bet," I nodded. I had little doubt Ray was telling me the truth. I considered what motivated the sudden, drunken confession. He wanted me to like him. He wanted my respect.

"My real talent was making bombs," he boasted. He was definitely on a roll now. "I could take simple light switches and turn them into mercury timers. You set the switch under a car, fused to a quarter, half a pound of C-4 plastic explosive, and depending on the angle of the switch, the car will explode from a bump in the highway or when it comes to a sudden stop."

He laughed, watching me, hoping he was making an impression. He was, although I did my best not to show it.

"One day I'll get bored, and for old time's sake I'll do you a favor."

"How's that?"

"We'll go out together and get rid of someone you'd rather not have on this planet."

I studied the boyish face of this short, stocky creature and the intelligent eyes darting nervously behind his glasses. I saw him as the undervalued outsider, turning his rejection into the lethal skills of a contract killer. It took balls, I had to give him that much. He was neither Rambo nor the Terminator, but an actual bad ass in a world of frauds. I was vaguely flattered he wanted to be my friend.

At the same time I realized the other shoe was dropping— a fervent stomp, echoing among the canyons. First Louis, and now Ray were confiding in me like I was their kindred spirit. I had crossed over their threshold and passed all the tests. Now I was ready for membership in their secret circle. Trouble was, I was never much of a joiner.

Ray departed not long after, and with the party reduced to a few drunken stragglers, I figured I had done my duty for Noah Brown. In the din of fading festivity I made my way to Louis' bedroom to grab my jacket and say goodnight. I knocked perfunctorily and opened the door. Instead of the usual warm embrace and hearty farewell, I walked into an ice-cold silence and an ambiance so intense with fear and embarrassment it was all I could do not to turn and leave. About ten grim faced men were spread around the room, sitting on the bed, squatting on the floor.

Louis was sitting in his desk chair that was turned away from his desk. He had his elbows on his thighs, and his head hung low like a dog that had been whipped into subservience. He was solemn and trembling, the center of the attention not as the host but as the condemned. He barely acknowledged my presence, never daring to look at me.

As I quickly adjusted to the startling and sickening ambiance, I noticed the cause of anxiety was an attractive Chinese woman in her middle thirties. She was well dressed in tan tweed designer slacks and a white silk blouse. Her lustrous dark hair fell to her shoulders. She could have been an executive, a rich Asian housewife, or an actress who wandered in by mistake. But there was no mistake, or if there was, poor Louis had made it. It was incredible that among a roomful of macho gun guys, she was in total command.

She stood scowling over Louis, her hands on her hips. She glanced at me indifferently, before turning back to him. I gathered from the look on her face, her indifference was less for my benefit than it was for the others in the room. She was demonstrating that my sudden presence meant nothing to her. From her body language, I realized she had been reading Louis the riot act. It was no ordinary scolding, but a methodical act of intimidation that had reduced him to a quivering mess. She focused her eyes on the back of his head as if to make him submit by sheer force of will.

If any situation in life was none of my business, this was certainly it. I watched fascinated and sickened as she continued to stare and he continued to tremble, his head bowing lower as a show of even greater subservience. I said nothing as I backed out the door.

I wasn't home an hour when I heard a knock at my door. I had been drifting off in the bedroom, and the sudden intrusion sent chicken skin chills from my throat to my sphincter. Tasha, my always loyal but often condescending Briard, even gave me a funny look, as if to ask, "Who the hell's knocking at four in the morning?"

As Tasha ran off barking, my first thought was that Louis and the boys had decided they could do without any witnesses to their recent psychodrama. I grabbed my Colt .45, the pistol Louie recommended for home defense, and crept down the hallway toward the front door. Noah was peeking impatiently through the glass window.

"How was the party?" he asked me, after requesting coffee and sitting down at the kitchen table. I watched him dump his usual three teaspoons of sugar into his mug.

"A lot of bad dancing."

He glowered half in play. He knew I was fucking with him, but his face let me know his patience would only hold out so long.

"I walked in on Louie being roasted over the coals by a Chinese woman. You should have seen it, like a scene right out of the Manchurian Candidate. You know, Louie all bent and bowed in total submission. It was so weird. Sickening, really."

Noah's jaw dropped momentarily. His show of surprise was startling to me, since Noah usually revealed nothing of his emotions. By comparison, this subtle tip off was as glaring a display as a white trash celebration over winning the Publisher's Clearing House Sweepstakes.

"When it was time to say goodnight, I walked into Louie's bedroom, and there was this good looking Chinese woman standing over Louie, giving him absolute hell."

"How could you tell she was giving him hell?"

"Couldn't miss it. They way she was standing over him with her hands on her hips. The vibe in the room was so thick you could have cut it with a knife. And there was poor fucking Louie, bent over just like I told you, in total submission. But you know what?"

"You tell me."

"Deep down inside, I sensed that Louie somehow enjoyed it. Nothing really concrete, just vibes that there was almost a sexual rush about it that was somehow turning him on. A dominatrix in tweed instead of black leather."

"What were the others doing?"

"The other guys? Sitting around all glum and silent. Afraid, really. I felt that this wasn't the first time they had seen this performance. Again that's just a guess, but I don't think I'm wrong."

"Can you tell the difference between Japanese and Chinese?"

"Of course."

"The Chinese woman. You never saw her there before?"

"Never."

"Could you identify her, if you had to?"

"Yeah. Sure. What's this about?"

Noah shrugged me off. "It's about fighting a war that lasts over centuries. You never really win it; you just try to make the other guy lose. C'mon," he gestured. "Take a ride with me."

chapter

SEVEN

Noah drove his Corvette up Beverly Glen and along Mulholland Drive, until he found a vacant parking spot overlooking the city. Down below, the lights of the city shimmered before us, aglow in the allure and promise of a different world and better times. Small wonder this part of Mulholland Drive had served for years as lover's lane. Only now, with all the wanton construction, the remaining vacant spaces were rapidly disappearing. Instead of teenagers parked in their cars, looking for romance, estate size monstrosities had filled in nearly all the vacant spaces. No more love on lover's lane. Just excess. And Noah and I.

"You said with the Chinese woman he sat with his head bowed and didn't say a word?"

I nodded. "Pretty unsettling. Especially with all the others in the room."

"Do you believe Louie's stories? About killing people?"

I nodded. "At first I thought he was full of shit, but I have had a serious change of mind. Something about him, and the way he tells the same stories over and over. They never vary the way they would if all of it was fantasy."

"You pick up on that?" he asked with a hint of admiration.

"Well, I was a journalist. You pay attention to that kind of thing."

Noah paused, lighting a cigarette. As a show of courtesy he cracked his window, exhaling a long, steady stream into the cool night air. The look on his face made me believe he had reached a major decision. He had.

"I've been keeping a file on Louie since the day he first moved into that house. I tracked him and watched him, observed his friends and, like he said, I bugged his house and the telephone lines."

Noah squinted at me, openly gauging my reaction. Satisfied I wasn't preparing to leap from the car, he went on.

"The reason I didn't go to the party? I met with my peers, and they decided I better stay away. We weren't really sure what the gun nuts had in mind; only that the party was a setup for someone to meet me. Now it is obvious. Louie had promised to deliver me to the Chinese woman, so she could have a crack at persuading me to roll over and work for their side."

I felt the unmistakable chill of truth running up my spine.

"Like I said, I've been tracking this for years now. From time to time I had other federal agents come to the house and establish surveillance. They'd take a look at Louie and friends for a couple of days and then pass them off as fantasy dwellers. Harmless gun nuts."

Noah laughed in recollection and took another drag on his cigarette. For sure as hell, I wasn't going anywhere. He could take all the time he wanted.

"My own credibility was being questioned. One time they had me in for psychological tests. They thought I was maybe losing it over Louie."

"C'mon."

"The night of the party we had surveillance all over the house. Somehow we missed the Chinese woman. I don't know how she got in or how she got out without being detected. Probably in the trunk of a car. But you saw her, that's the important thing."

"She was hard to miss."

"She was the piece we've been looking for. I always suspected Louie was up to something, but I couldn't tell whom he was tied in with. That woman you saw? A dollar to a soggy doughnut, she's an agent for the People's Republic of China. And that's the giveaway. She was giving him hell because Louie failed to get me to come to the party. He had failed in his mission, and she was all pissed off."

"So what are you saying?" I asked.

"Louie is a Chinese mole. He's probably been active for many years."

He took a final drag on his cigarette and flicked it out the window. Fire hazards were the least of his concerns.

"Louie. The others. Most are part of a network. How big it is, it's hard to say. But we'll find out. That I can promise you."

"Well," I said. "There's a reason you're telling me all this."

Noah smiled. "Let's face it; you love this kind of thing. You've been flirting with it in one way or another for your entire life.

"You're smart, so you got away with things. Things that maybe you shouldn't have been doing. But now it's time to contribute. It's time you did something for your country, don't you think? You know these people almost as well as I do. And you know they're dangerous. They're traitors."

"You want me to stay close to Louie? Is that it?"

"There are things I could teach you. Things I'll guarantee you'll never learn from anyone else. Let's face it; I'm nearly crippled. I need a good pair of legs. I could use your help, if you are willing to give it."

"And if not?"

His scowl belied his answer. "Then that's up to you."

I sighed and looked out over Los Angeles. I remembered all the movies I'd watched as a kid that were filmed not far from this very same spot. I remembered, as a young man, yearning to come to California and take in this view. I remembered driving up alone, staring out at the lights, the grids, the airplanes flashing overhead, and relishing the aura of promise offered by the city below. I loved it up there. It was a holy place. It was a living homage to the fading dream of carefree California. It was a fitting site for this defining moment. If I was embarking on the E-ticket ride into the shadow world of spying and intrigue, then it was poetic that this would be my point of departure.

chapter

EIGHT

In all my years prior to meeting Noah Brown, I paid little attention to the ubiquitous telephone lines strung across our world. Even the more obvious lines that were strung from pole to pole, I took for granted like most other people. If anything, save for visiting birds or discarded sneakers marking drug territory, telephone lines were never points of revelation, but parallel obstructions of the local vistas. Prior to my time with Noah Brown, I don't believe I once counted how many wires ran from the junction boxes on telephone poles to the millions of houses and buildings wired up for modern communication.

But now, with Noah Brown, I was receiving a crash course in phone line study. With Noah's prodding, I was suddenly aware of the bristling antennas on vans and trucks, and the actual number of telephone lines running into houses and even commercial buildings. We stood at roadside or climbed atop buildings, positioned ourselves strategically in order to count suspect cables and wires.

"You start to see a bunch of them entering a house or a small building," said Noah, "and you know, usually, someone's making their living the old fashioned way. They're stealing. Look over there."

We were standing on the edge of Mulholland Drive, where the narrow side street to Noah's house merged with the larger, winding highway that ran through the Santa Monica Mountain Range. His finger pointed down the road, across Mulholland, to the corner of another side street, where a couple dozen phone lines drooped from the junction box and ran into a compound of houses surrounded by eight foot cyclone fences topped with concertina wire. Various cars and trucks, mostly older and dusty, were parked in the gravel parking area just outside the fence.

"Right across the street," he commented. "Right up here in Beverly Hills. You could drive past here a thousand times and never notice it. If you pay attention, now and then you'll see someone patrolling with a guard dog on the leash. Can't tell me nothing's going on inside there. And I'll bet it's related to Louie and this whole other business."

"Like how?"

Twenty minutes later we were standing inside a noted real estate office where Wade, a longtime friend of Noah's, worked as one of the million brokers that fed off of Los Angeles. Wade, balding, sixty and eager to help, led us to the topographical charts where every house and every owner in the general area was listed. Like three scholars standing around the Scriptures, we traced the streets on the oversized charts until we came upon the compound.

"The Roberts Trust," Noah announced, smiling. "Sounds fishy already." He looked down again. "The trust has owned the property since 1963."

He sighed, removing his handkerchief to clean his glasses. "I'll bet this Roberts proves to be one interesting dude."

Noah thanked Wade and, in his slow and deliberate shuffle, made for the door.

"Twenty phone lines in a barbed wire compound and guard dogs. What do you think they are up to, exactly?"

"We'll find out soon enough."

Two nights later I joined Noah as a group of federal agents alighted from an assortment of vehicles the government had confiscated over the years. The agents were dressed casually, and many sported beards and jeans. Most were driving compact pickup trucks or sleek, Japanese imports that had been seized during a drug raid or appropriated because of tax fraud. Each agent carried a bag in hand or a sack over his shoulder. Each agent had a different assignment, whether it was bugging the phone lines, putting listening devices around the house or conducting surveillance of the premises. It wasn't at all like the movies where the federal agents are turned into bumbling caricatures. These guys moved quickly and efficiently, taking pictures, using special film for darkness.

I watched them skulking through the crisp night air, hardly making a sound. Lamplight glowed in the windows of surrounding houses, and occasionally a car passed by on Mulholland Drive. I wondered how many times a year the feds engaged in operations similar to this one. Operations you never heard about.

"Are you enjoying yourself?" Noah asked me.

I nodded. "Except I wish I was out there, working with them. Be kind of fun."

"I was one of the best at it," Noah lamented. He stretched out his legs, showing off his usual footwear—chukka boots with a plain-bottomed rubber sole. "Until my legs gave out."

Forty minutes later the operation was over, and Noah and I headed for Santo Pietro's pizza joint at the Glen Centre.

"The name of this game," he pronounced between bites of a medium cheese pizza, "is to make myself available. Put myself out there, and let them come to me. You," he laughed, "can keep me company."

"Now there's a job description. Company keeper."

"Seriously," he said, wiggling his ass in his chair, which was his custom as he made his way to the bottom line of any conversation. It was his tell, his inadvertent warning that the next thing out of his mouth would not be to your liking. "We may need to use you as a witness."

"A witness?" I felt the chill run over me.

He nodded. "To testify against Louie and the boys."

"It's not happening. I wouldn't do that."

"Why not?" he insisted, getting upset.

"It's one of those things. I won't let myself be used that way. It's far too easy to be left holding the trick bag. Not that it's ever happened before," I said, the sarcasm absolutely dripping. "But when it does fuck up, I don't want to have to duck into some witness protection program. I'm not built for small town life and franchise dining."

"I wouldn't do that to you."

"Yes you would, if you had to. Look, the best way not to end up disillusioned is to have no illusions to begin with. Things do go wrong, and it wouldn't be the first time that someone like me was hung out to dry."

Noah fumed, rubbing his thumbs together. "Then you know if you don't cooperate as a witness, you can't be involved in any of this."

"If that's the way it has to be..." I said, letting my voice trail off. I was angry now. "What do you think, you're banishing me from the prom? Fuck the prom! I didn't go to the prom either."

Noah and I made small talk for the rest of the night, until I dropped him off at his house. When he got out of the car, he started to say something but thought better of it. I didn't hear from him again for the better part of two weeks, which in my mind meant my new career as a spook was over before it began.

Just as well. I'd miss my relationship with Noah; that much I knew. But I also realized that was part of Noah's game—ingratiate himself and then withdraw. I was sure he assumed if left abandoned, I would accede to his demands. I would crave his companionship and feel I was missing out on his promise of adventure. Or perhaps he wanted to see if I was spiteful enough to go running pissed off to Louie and the gang, telling all I knew. I realized Noah's behavior said more about him and the people he worked with than it did about me. Hell would freeze over before I gave in.

Strangely, it was Louie, and not Noah, who two weeks later was the first to show up at my door. He was bearing a gift, a leather magazine holder that accommodated two semi-automatic clips and was designed to fit snugly in the back pocket of a pair of Levi's. Several months earlier, offhandedly, I had admired

Louie's. Now he brought me one of my own. Louie had a friend, a custom holster maker, who made them for his clients.

"Thanks."

"Elliot does such good work," he said, admiring the clip holder. "He's like an old time artisan master of his trade. You ought to get him to make you a shoulder holster."

I nodded, alarmed by his awkwardness. Louie was on a fishing expedition. His body language gave it away. That and the fact that he had never before visited my house.

"So where have you been keeping yourself?" he wanted to know.

"I've had work up to here. It's the kind of tedious crap that wears me out. It's like, picture doing a hundred fillings in a row."

"I'd rather not," he laughed.

"Hey, you want a beer?"

"Sure."

"Any kind in particular?"

"As long as it's cold."

I went to retrieve his beer. When I returned to the living room, Louie was on his feet, shuffling toward the door.

"Gotta get going," he said, as if he had forgotten he had asked for a beer.

"What about this?" I asked, handing him the bottle.

He accepted it reluctantly, took a few quick swigs and handed it back. "I forgot that beer makes me sleepy when I drink it in the afternoon."

I nodded, as if he made sense. "Okay."

Like that, Louie was gone.

Three days later, with no warning and no phone call, Noah showed up. I almost wondered if they were double teaming me in some weird gaslight conspiracy they had cooked up over a neighborly barbecue.

"You've got to start calling me before you come over," I scolded. "I could have people here. The kind who might find our association more than a little...awkward."

"So what's the big deal if I meet your friends?"

It was my turn to look at him with sheer indulgence. We had had this conversation several times before. I decided rather than explain it again, I'd ignore him.

"Anyway, what brings you here?"

He sighed, sat down on my sofa and carefully surveyed the room. "Put the TV on," he ordered. "But turn down the sound."

I obeyed his instructions. Noah clapped. Waited. And then clapped again.

"See that?" he whispered.

"What?"

He pointed to the TV. "That white line," he said as he clapped again.

"Yeah?"

He scribbled a word on a piece of paper. Bug.

"You're fucking with me?"

He shook his head, no.

He had just confirmed a haunting feeling of mine that the walls, indeed, had ears.

"I have to go to the car a minute," he said, excusing himself.

Moments later he was back inside the house, a black suitcase in hand. He unpacked a few tools, earphones and a couple of electronic pieces. He slipped on the earphones and kneeled down in front of my home entertainment unit. Carefully he fiddled with the radio receiver, a quizzical look on his face. He kept referring to some electronic device that was no larger than a two-slice toaster. Soon he smiled faintly, nodded to himself in confirmation of something only he knew. I could tell he was truly enjoying himself.

"Just like I thought," he said, packing up his gear. "They set the frequency between two FM radio stations. I fixed it so all it will do is transmit static. They'll probably think there's something wrong with the bug itself. Sometime this week I'll send some people over, and they can pull it from the house."

"The question is—who stuck it there?" I felt a new type of chill running through me.

"Louie. He was over here, wasn't he?"

"How did you know?"

"Are you forgetting? I'm bugging his phones."

Made sense.

Noah shrugged like it was no big deal. "The real question is not who planted the bug, but to where is it transmitting? One of this quality could transmit all the way up to Mulholland. To the fortress."

"You mean the house across Mulholland? The one that's part of the Roberts Trust?"

"Oh," Noah said, as if it was an afterthought. Surely it wasn't. The feigned afterthought was a means to needle me about my recent exclusion. "They're running insurance scams out of the fortress. That's why the radio repeater is on site. It was the same kind of repeater they wanted to put up at Louie's, some years ago. That is, until the boys found out what I did for a living."

"So, this repeater. What's it about?"

"Say there's an accident, right? There's a need for adjusters, and as often as not the insurance adjusters are independents—they work for themselves. So whenever there's a fire or an accident, the claim goes out over radio. That house intercepts the signal, and they send out their own insurance adjuster, someone who is in with them. The adjuster gets his fee, and the fortress gets its rake off the top."

"What could that amount to?"

"Thirty, forty million a year. Maybe more. It's a big business, and you could support a lot of spying with that kind of dough. But it doesn't stop there. We've been bugging their faxes and computers..."

"You can do that?"

"By assessing the pulse rates," Noah assured me. "The Roberts Trust is actually a holding company for at least twenty-two legitimate businesses, most of which are involved in technology of some sort."

"Like what, computers?"

"Security systems, video equipment, all sorts of electronics. The oldest one is a video processing plant. It originally sold equipment to television stations. Some of the companies are subcontractors for the bigger defense outfits, like Lockheed. All seemingly legitimate companies, the oldest were established back as early as the fifties."

"So now they're reputable institutions."

"Yeah. Now here's the thing. Old man Roberts is a downed Navy flier, crippled and a POW during the Korean War. He gets around in a wheelchair. Does that remind you of anybody?"

"Yeah. What's his face? Louie's friend. Tom Raymond."

"Another downed flier. There's a third one living up the block from me. He keeps to himself."

"Lot of downed fliers in this episode. Look, if they're bugging me, then they're probably watching me. But why?"

"You've been keeping the wrong company," Noah laughed. "Me. They probably want to see what they can get out of you."

"But Louie would have told them that, right? Doesn't make sense."

"Maybe they're not all entirely connected to Louie. Maybe it's a separate group, working independently. I'll put some people around, see what's up. They'll keep an eye out on you."

"Thanks." I pondered how long someone, or a group of someone's, had been listening to everything in the house, tuning in to every intimate conversation, eavesdropping on sexual activities. I first assumed it was Louie who had planted the bug. Now I wondered if it was Noah's work. He could have done it so he could look like a hero, or to make amends for my upset over the witness business.

"Forget it," Noah was saying.

"Forget what?"

"Getting back at Louie. I know what you're thinking, and it'll only create a mess. The kind of mess that no one needs right now."

I smiled. He would have had a fit if he knew what I was really thinking.

"So now what?"

"I have to go to Nicaragua."

"Vacation or business?"

"Monsignor Erskine Kroll. Louie's friend. He visits his office from time to time. You ever meet him?"

"Yeah, as a matter of fact, I have."

"I think he might be ass deep in this business. So that means starting out by tracing his activities in Nicaragua and then working my way back through what I can find out about his past."

I smiled. "I think I can save you some airfare."

With Noah in tow, I retrieved from my garage the thirty-page biography that a year before I stuck into a cardboard file box and deposited unceremoniously onto my garage floor. At one point water seeped in, and the contents of the box ended up mildewed and crusty. I considered throwing out the box and its contents, but I didn't. You never know, I thought. It was one of the most fortunate decisions I could have made.

The insides of that mildewed box contained an equally mildewed copy of Monsignor Erskine Kroll's abbreviated biography. The good Monsignor had presented it to me a month after a meeting I had with Kroll and Louis at Louis' dental office.

"I want you to meet one of my oldest and most trusted friends," Louie had announced with considerable pride.

Kroll, it turned out, was actually a Bishop in the Old Holy Church. But wearing his powder blue golf shirt and funky, bargain chinos, he looked like a mix between the greeter at Wal-Mart and the gaunt, sallow skinned bank robbers who decorate post office walls. He had a flinty demeanor, and his sharp, beady eyes behind cheap bifocals were far more suspicious than those of any confessor-clergyman inured to the sins of humanity. I shook hands and found his grip was clammy and tentative. There was a trace aura of death about him, the kind of aura particular to low ranking mobsters or soldiers of fortune.

"What do you mean by the Old Holy Church?" I asked. I had no idea why he and Louis had been stressing the Old in Old Holy.

"I'm not Roman Catholic," he provided in what was for him a familiar explanation. "The Old Holy Church is sometimes known as the First Holy Church. We view ourselves somewhat like medieval Catholics. And we don't recognize the Vatican."

"I see," I nodded in understanding. I didn't really, but I was in no mood for theological controversy.

Louis proclaimed Erskine a hero of sorts, for opposing the Sandinistas in their overthrow of the Somoza regime in Nicaragua.

"He risked his life," beamed Louis, basking in the glow of a genuine hero.

At Louie's prompting, the Bishop claimed he worked alongside what he termed the democratic forces in trying to prevent the Sandinistas from taking control of the government. With Louis' help he smuggled medical supplies into Nicaragua and tended the wounded with homeopathic remedies. It was a losing proposition. He had been arrested and beaten but was fortunate enough to find refuge inside the German Embassy until he could arrange for his escape.

"Now I'm back in the States," Kroll explained. "I'm making people aware of the corruption and violation of civil rights. I attend a lot of seminars and fundraisers. Not long ago I addressed the House of Representatives' Central American Appropriations Committee about the evolving Sandinista problem."

"Wouldn't this make a wonderful movie?" Louis beamed.

No, it wouldn't, I thought, but kept that thought to myself. These two had no idea the majority of the politically liberal Hollywood community viewed the Sandinistas as revolutionary heroes. Not only was his unpopular side of the cause, but Monsignor Kroll had come up a loser, and losers made rotten heroes for a Movie of the Week.

"Tell you what," I said to Monsignor Kroll. "What you describe sounds somewhat interesting, but it's a complex story and difficult to follow. The best thing you can do is write out your story in maybe thirty pages, and then I'll look it over and see where we can go from there."

I never believed Erskine Kroll would actually sit down and write his story. I was wrong. Six weeks later Monsignor Kroll handed me the abbreviated tale of his life, along with a series of religious tracts he had written. The tracts were rambling justifications for the use of force and validation for Monsignor Kroll's obscure political visions. As one who is turned off by dogma, I barely made it through a quick perusal of the tracts. The biography I found a little more interesting, although after reading through it, I didn't think much of Monsignor Kroll's life. As I had first surmised, he was certainly not a cinematic hero.

Now Noah and I were sitting around my kitchen table leafing through the moldy pages.

"It's basically some pathetic, half-assed, self-analytical drivel about a lost man living in a sad world, desperate to find meaning in his dreadful experience. Nothing close to what I'd expect from a cleric.

"Goes on about all kinds of stuff. Look how he puts 'third draft' up at the top of the page. He really gave this thing some thought."

We read carefully how Kroll was born in 1931 in Camden, New Jersey, to what he described as a family of historical prominence and modern genteel poverty. He wrote of his early education in Drexel Hill, a Philadelphia suburb; the name of which he spelled incorrectly. He reflected on his intermittent life in the resort town of Cape May, New Jersey, and on a farm in upstate Pennsylvania. He categorized himself as a classic underachiever, and his German influences were a product of his environment, including membership in the Liederkrantz, a beer drinking and singing society. I couldn't picture it. Kroll was not the type.

Kroll left home, disappointed, disillusioned by what life had to offer, and he served in the Air Force. Upon discharge, he moved to New Orleans, where he found a "richly diverse and creative set of people, all brilliant, all at odds with the world." In the fifties he kicked around for a while, ending up in Southern California, a student of homeopathy.

Eventually he turned to the Old Holy Church and was ordained as a priest in 1965. He advanced to Bishop, and a few years after being ordained he founded Divinity House, a refuge for orphaned children. Over these years he also continued to perform medical research.

"What do you think?" asked Noah, after we finished reading the document.

"He's not from Philly, I can tell you that much. The way he talks and acts. Not the Mid-Atlantic cleric type at all."

Noah smiled approvingly. "You know how many of these guys are living in the USA? More than seventy thousand citizens of the world are living in this country, all with fictitious backgrounds, bogus life stories. This is one of them," he announced, waving the Bishop's bio. "At this point in my life I can smell it. And you know what else?"

I didn't. He went on.

"When there's one, there's always a bunch of fellow travelers," he assured me, using a term I hadn't heard used sincerely in quite some time.

"There's always some truth in the best of lies, but I'd be surprised if anything less than three quarters of this wasn't pure bullshit."

"Look." Noah pointed out one paper that was supposedly signed by Somoza, former dictator of Nicaragua. "His signature is nothing but a rubber stamp.

"See where he writes about studying homeopathy and attending to the wounded Sandinistas. He tended to them, alright, with poison created from his homeopathy learning. He probably killed more Sandinistas than any sharpshooter. There has to be some German linkage, if the Germans were willing to get him out of there."

"So what about his big anti-communist posture? That feels like it's real. The way he talks about communists; it's with genuine disdain."

"What most people don't realize is that revolution was a three-ring circus. Somoza was Somoza, and the Russians supported the Sandinistas. A third group was Chinese influenced. Little is known about them, but they were there. My hunch is the good Bishop was one of them.

"I'm going to have to check this out," Noah sighed in weary resignation. "Feel like a trip to New Orleans?"

chapter

NINE

I soon was to learn that Noah's out of town trips were almost always by car. Except for quick excursions to Washington, or overseas, Noah preferred slouching toward Bethlehem in his white Corvette to the dubious rewards of modern commercial air travel. Although jets would get you there faster, people who checked guns on planes, especially federal agents, created a profile that was further complicated by inconvenience and easy recognition. Noah claimed there was no such thing as discretion when you traveled by air, and it was much harder to shake any tail, or prevent anyone from keying into your schedule.

"You travel by car, and you have other options."

"Like?"

"You can kill the sonofabitch and leave him in the middle of nowhere."

He was only half joking.

Noah allowed how he used invitations to scientific and technological conferences as fronts for the real business at hand. Trade shows and conventions provided excellent cover for actual operations.

"Always cover your bases the best you can. Anyone ever asks what you're doing; you're at the conference. Deniability, that's the main issue. Plausible deniability. Always build in your alibi up front, so you have time to get comfortable with the story. A trade show is an excellent front; it's the perfect meeting ground for friendly forces to get off and talk without anyone taking special notice."

Since there was no actual conference scheduled for New Orleans that week, we snuck out of town under cover of darkness and blasted out across the California desert before Dr. Louie could take note of our absence. By the time we had passed through three states I had determined from his views that Noah was a bonafide reactionary. He was overly paranoid and lacking tolerance for social and ethnic diversity. I saw him clinging to a kind of paranoia that justified his own existence and that of the agencies he served.

In return, Noah viewed me as a perennial scofflaw. I was a world of potential gone astray, a product of that boomer generation, with little appreciation for the existing social and moral values. It was my very quest for personal freedom that had put our nation in peril.

His obstruction of social progress and my threat to social stability at least provided us with a reference point, a fair beginning to our advancing relationship. In the course of our sometimes heated discussions, we had also reached an agreement concerning my aborted career as a witness and my related duties for Noah.

"Tell me. This witness business. Are we over that yet? Otherwise, here's how it'll play. I'll be forever challenged to escape it, and you'll always be thinking what you have to do to get me into that witness chair. Either way, it's a waste of time."

"I figured that."

I stared incredulously.

"I mean it. Forget it. Let's move on."

"Missed me, huh?" I teased. "Just couldn't stay away."

He frowned in disdain but wasn't about to argue.

"I'll pay you out of pocket, pick up your expenses, and you'll work as my personal assistant. Mind you, you're not officially part of the government project. You work for me, privately. You get killed, and it's your own tough luck. No insurance."

On the long drive to New Orleans Noah talked about his kids and about his wife, who was killed in an auto accident back in the fifties. He didn't favor his kids, particularly, and from what I gathered, they were far removed from worshipping Daddy.

"I was tough," he acknowledged. "What with all the drugs and other nonsense in the LA schools, I was hard on them. My two sons, especially. Gave them lots of projects."

"I'll bet you did."

He looked at me sternly. "I can't say I don't regret some of it. I was probably too hard on them. Some of what I did was probably pretty awful, especially by today's standards. But they turned out okay. My eldest daughter is an attorney; my eldest son is an engineer. My youngest son was in the FBI for a while, but he just resigned after spending two years undercover. He's starting accounting class. And my youngest girl, well she teaches school. She's still a little bit of a problem."

Noah laughed. "I remember one time when she was little. I had been away so long. We had slipped from Afghanistan into China, across the mountain ranges. You think it is spooky now; you should've seen it back then. It was like the sixteenth century.

"I was assigned to plant listening devices along the Chinese border, so we'd know if the Chinese were moving troops against India. I must've been gone for eight months at least. When I showed up at the door, she started crying."

"She missed you?"

"Naw, she didn't recognize me. Thought I was a stranger. I scared her with my beard growth and all."

"They have any kids of their own?"

He shook his head. I could see this was a sore spot.

"No, no," he sighed. "I told them they were just plain afraid to have kids."

Or too scarred from what I imagined was Noah's draconian child raising style. I had seen a photo of him, taken back in the fifties—prime commie hunting time. Noah, at his physical peak, was leaning against a rail somewhere, wearing his suspicious scowl and the buzz cut hairstyle favored by hard heads all over the world. He was the archetypal tough guy in the gray flannel suit. Johnny G-Man! Ready to take on any mission that promised to raise the adrenalin. Family and children were probably a mere formality, a nod to civics and society. Even the spiffy haircut was all part of that old fashioned myth branded our way of life, reinforcing the spoon-fed belief that you were a good guy in a great country, and that, despite the covert ops and the illegitimate destruction of legitimate governments and social organizations; you were imbued with nobility and sense of purpose.

For a guy like Noah, at least the Noah in the fifties photo, plumbing the gray areas of morality and legitimacy was necessary in order to enforce a world of black and white. The ambiguous gestures were the bedrock of the absolutes we, as a society, had once upon a time so richly believed in. Back then it was rare for a man of his beliefs, of his fiber, to dare explore the dark side of his career choice, the deadly Cold War Carnival where his demons found purchase.

But that was then, and this was now. I saw that the older Noah, like the citizens he had sworn to serve and protect, was beginning to question the virtue of his actions and the actual meaning of his life. Now that mortality was finally staring him square in the face, purpose had shades of gray.

Despite his position, wealth and experience, he found he possessed more questions than answers. This was why I was around, why he needed me. Louie and a gang of Chinese spies he could handle by himself. I was more than the willing student. Despite all his accusations, I was a part of modern culture, a culture of relative morality and a mutable national pride. I was part of the permissive culture that men like Noah didn't understand. I was a mutant outgrowth of the old American ethic, an accidental byproduct of Noah's world of absolutes. I was cast by fate to learn from his experiences and listen to his story. And, oddly enough, I was there to provide validation for him when our journey had ended.

chapter

TEN

Loretta Bouchet had spent a good part of her eighty-nine years tucked away in the northeastern section of New Orleans's French Quarter, or Vieux Carre as some still called it. She lived several blocks from the Esplanade and the Old U.S. Mint in one of the well worn residential sections of the Quarter, in a neighborhood that welcomed few tourists. A scant mile from the wild carousing found on Bourbon Street, the cobbled streets evoked an eerie solitude.

I felt the Quarter's age. Its colorful history was astonishingly evident in the peeling pastel walls and old brick courtyards, the weathered porches, and in the fancy ironwork that was sweaty from the recent drizzle. I could smell the river and the thick, moist dankness found only in a city below sea level. It wasn't difficult on these quiet side streets to envision a time when the French Quarter was as elegant as it was wild. I thought of the Bishop walking these crooked sidewalks and wondered what his thoughts were as he traipsed through the world of Tennessee Williams.

As it turned out, Loretta Bouchet was able to answer some of those questions, especially those that Noah posed with seductive grace and authority. She still lived on the first floor of a three-story building she owned. We had followed the trail Kroll left through municipal records, and we had visited three other places, knocking on doors in dark, stuffy hallways and climbing squeaking stairs to no avail. And then we lucked out with Mrs. Bouchet. Years ago Mrs. Bouchet had been a performer, bumping and grinding in the clubs on Bourbon Street. She had married, living well until her husband took up with a woman in Houston and disappeared from her life. Now she was just another old woman in a faded housedress, scuffed shoes and an ill-fitting denture plate that created a lot of sloshing and spittle when she talked. Fortunately, she still had her memory and most of her marbles. It was with great pride that Mrs. Bouchet took us on an obligatory tour of her scrapbook and collection of photos. She highlighted the moment by serving us stale almond cookies and Luzianne tea.

"Here. Here," she said, pointing to an old photo of a young Erskine Kroll standing with his cronies out on the sidewalk. "This was Erskine and the bunch of them. He lived on the third floor. Here's me. I was pretty then," she sighed in amazement.

"The boys were nice enough. A little too quiet, and a little strange, I would guess," she said, her dentures making slushy sounds so "guess" came out as "guesh." "Strange, even for New Orleans."

"Kroll here, I remember him always with an odd looking young man. The two were not at all a handsome couple."

"Were they gay, Mrs. Bouchet? Homosexual?"

She paused, closing her eyes, remembering. "In those days people weren't as open with such things. "But if I had to guess, I'd say it was pretty mixed bunch. Some were. Some weren't.

"Look at these photos," prompted Noah. Among them were photos of Louie as a younger man. "You know him?"

"Yeah, he was here. Only not all the time. He'd come, stay for a while and then he was off to somewhere. If memory serves, Erskine traveled some, too. He'd be gone for weeks, months even. Don't know where though. Never asked, and he never told me.

"They all, the group of them, used to hang down at some coffee house, but that's been closed for years. The bar, though, the Sacred Horn. I think was the name of it. That's still open." She laughed. "An old codger runs it."

The Sacred Horn was an obscure hole in the wall on a side street that stank of piss and beer and the petro-chemicals wafting off the river. Officially, the building was a hotel, with the bar downstairs and a half a dozen rooms or so perched on the three stories above. I guessed the rooms were rented out to a mix of businessmen, hustlers, and anyone else who had the time to subscribe to mutual consent for an hour or two.

Garner Shockley owned the place, and like Loretta claimed, he was an old codger clinging to the looks and mannerisms of a fallen patrician. Shockley was still trim, and he had a full head of curly white hair that, judging by its length, he was clearly proud of. He wore a white button down oxford shirt under a flea market pale blue blazer and wrinkled khakis. He smoked unfiltered cigarettes with yellow stained fingers and sipped from a short beer, a drink born by cautious alcoholics dragging one leg from the wagon.

"What can I do for y'all?" he smiled. He posted a wary, monarchial sneer to convey he was pretty well connected with the scions of the Crescent City, so don't fuck with him. Like sharks, blowfish or the meager chameleon, this was his pathetic version of the survival instinct nature had afforded.

"Mr. Shockley," Noah began.

Shockley nodded, stubbing a cigarette on his plank wooden floor. "That's me. Who are you?"

"Do you have an office, or some place we can talk?"

"You ain't cops. I know all the cops around here. And besides, you're Yankees."

"Actually I'm more of a Dodgers fan," I told him.

Shockley knitted his brow and laughed good-naturedly. He cast his eyes down at my shoes and assessed the cut of my clothes. Satisfied I wasn't totally the peasant, he nodded almost imperceptibly, exhaling a thick plume of smoke through his nose. He squinted at Noah and then looked back at me.

"Maybe you're something else altogether?"

"Maybe you don't want to know who we are," Noah answered.

"Just what I was thinking."

"You're thinking right," Noah assured him. "I know you can handle the local authorities, but all those federal issues, it can be tough trying to handle them."

His flushing red face let us know Shockley was doing a poor job of hiding his fear. "Let's go to my office, where we'll have a little privacy."

What Shockley called an office was a dimly lit cubbyhole, dominated by an old wooden desk. The desk was piled high with papers, and the papers were piled high with dust. There were a couple of shelves and an old steel cabinet, which stood beside an ancient doorway. It looked like dead flies, rat shit and dirt supported the old plaster walls.

"Leads back to the storeroom," he said, when he caught me eyeing the doorway. "Ain't nothing there but boxes of liquor and a sleepy old tomcat. Catches his mice back in there. Have a look if you want."

Noah whipped out his pictures and laid them on the desk. "You recognize any of these characters? I know it's been awhile."

"Forty years, damn near," Shockley snorted in near disbelief. "What's this about? The Kennedy thing again?"

"What Kennedy thing?"

"The assassination. You know, the President. JFK."

"What makes you say that?" Noah asked with renewed interest.

Shockley tapped the photos. "Some of these boys, they were friends with David Ferrie. Remember him? The nut job Jim Garrison pegged as a suspect in the conspiracy he couldn't prove. Mind you, I don't know what's true that way and what isn't. Don't care much, neither."

Silence passed between us as Shockley eyed us more closely. "You're not here about Kennedy," he said with piqued interest. "What's this about then? If it ain't about Kennedy?"

Noah shrugged. "Just a little game of hide and seek."

Shockley nodded dubiously. "You play hide n' seek with these boys, you'd better be carrying more n' flashlight."

"Characters, huh?"

"More than that," he announced in a pure Southern drawl, tapping the photographs. "They were living in a different world. They used to play soldier with Ferrie and them anti-commies back in early sixties. Out by the lake sometimes. But mostly down in the Delta. Thought they were going to take back Cuba, or some such nonsense. That was until the federal agents closed them down. Afterward, a lot of them just up and disappeared."

"Were all of them involved?"

Shockley looked at the pictures again and then up at us. "You boys watch where you're stepping. There's still a snake or two under those rocks."

We had dinner at Felix's on Iberville St., a casual deli-meets-oyster-bar kind of place that'd been there for years. We sat in a corner booth, and over the din of the crowded oyster bar we discussed what we had learned so far.

"I'm going to have to see Garrison," Noah decided while eating oysters and nursing a beer. "His old Kennedy files could turn up something."

"About Kennedy? I'd love to know about that."

He shook me off. "Let's get this straight right now. We're not here for Kennedy."

"Still," I started to protest.

He held up his hand as a sign he wouldn't have the patience to listen. "This kind of investigation always leads through all kinds of bad dudes and criminal situations. None of which have to do with any of our priorities. At best, we take notes and pass it on. Sometimes we even ignore it. The only time we really follow the lead is if it leads us to bigger pay dirt.

"You understand me? Because I can't have you wrestling with the Kennedy business. We take what we came here for, and then we move on."

"When are you going to see Garrison?"

He waved his fork at me. "When I do, I'll see him alone."

"So we're in this together, only not all the time?"

Noah smiled. "That's how we play this game. We compartmentalize. You know what you need to know."

The following midnight I found myself in the French Market at the Café Du Monde, sipping coffee and eating beignets. I was to meet Noah there. It was the kind of balmy night Southerners like to brag about in song and romance, so I didn't mind waiting for Noah in the legendary outdoor café. Two women sat down at the opposite table and attempted to flirt with me. Judging by their awkward enthusiasm, at first I speculated they were recent divorcees out on the kind of sex spree that so often follows the ordeal of a lousy marriage. I smiled politely and turned my attention to my order of hot beignets.

Fifteen minutes later Noah hobbled in, taking it slow and steady as he shuffled around the tables. Despite all his will and determination, I realized a sudden misstep and he could be dumped on the ground. But this ugly reality, like his crippled legs and humped back, Noah accepted without complaint. Still, there were times I feared I had cast my fate with a fragile old man.

"I see you've been busy," he joked, head gesturing to the two women sitting across from me.

"The divorcees? I was saving them for you."

"I like the short one. I need a good toilet. Otherwise they can't really accommodate me. I was blessed," he said when he saw the puzzled look on my face.

"What are you talking about, toilet?"

"Larger in the rear end. You never heard the term, toilet?"

"Yeah. Kohler makes them in decorator colors. Never heard it used for a woman's ass. Maybe it's a generational thing," I offered in conciliation, having noted his embarrassment. "And what do you mean, blessed?"

Noah held his hands apart, as if to show me the size of his penis.

Blessed, I thought to myself, the irony notwithstanding. Noah had a hunched back, almost no use of his chicken legs, but a big penis. And so he felt blessed. A blessed troll.

"Time was I could do them two at a time," he lamented while ordering his coffee. "Now," he smiled, "I need a little inspiration."

"You have a good meeting?" I asked, interrupting his reverie.

He shrugged and signaled the waiter. "I told Garrison he was a better researcher than he was a detective. He has a fistful of clues and a pocket of wrong conclusions."

"What do you mean?"

Noah waited until the waiter had departed with his order. "He had a lot of his dudes pegged as rightwing crazies, when I think they were working for the other team. It's nothing new, really. The Soviet agents from the good old days, the Cold War, they would attempt to infiltrate a group by talking strong right wing philosophy when they were really Communists at heart. They did it with the unions, the trade organizations, even in the military."

"Like the Manchurian Candidate?"

Noah chuckled. "Yeah. It's how you attract the nut jobs. Look at the ones at Louie's soirees. Right wing. Left wing. Political doctrine doesn't matter to them. It's just being against the government that's important."

"The anti's?" I asked, drawing on a phrase that Noah often used to describe the rabid anti establishment individuals.

"Yeah. The anti's. They all hate the government for one reason or another, but it never constitutes a formal ideology. Just hating is enough. For all the weird reasons they can think of. And let's never forget the money. Take a guy like Louie; he's probably twenty percent ideology and eighty percent money. You hear him talk about how he hates the government and all the ways they have of controlling him. But it's the money that really drives his train. The money and the excitement.

"I figure the Bishop got to him years ago. Maybe he got to him in more ways than one."

"Like lovers?"

Noah raised his eyebrows. "Not a particularly pretty picture, the Bishop and Louie, but hey, love is blind, or at least nearsighted. The Bishop probably turned him and showed him how he could hate for profit."

"And the Bishop? It's not the money with him."

Noah sipped from his coffee mug and picked at his beignets. "No, he's a diehard. He is a true believer, which makes him a far more dangerous guy."

"So what have we learned, class, from our trip to New Orleans?"

"That the Bishop did his initial organizing down here among the handful of dangerous misfits who were running around with hangers on and renegade CIA agents. Louie, even then, was one of his acolytes. Here they were, pretending to be rabid right wing fanatics when, at heart, they were Maoist Commies."

I glanced over at the two divorcees who were staring back curiously. Suddenly it dawned on me that the two women weren't sex hungry divorcees, but federal agents who were keeping tabs on me. I studied their makeup, which was thick and uncertain, as if they were confusing cocktail hour with midnight coffee at Café Du Monde.

Their eyes told me they were far too smart to be that ignorant, and their preppie outfits hinted they were well bred products of east coast or southern universities. As for their thick, rubber-soled penny loafers, well if anything was the giveaway, the shoes were certainly it.

The more I stared, the more unsettled they became, shifting uncomfortably in their chairs. Their formerly overt flirting now lapsed into semi-embarrassed sidelong glances as they struggled to act cool. I took delight in their embarrassment, but felt a little sorry for them. Their covers were blown, their assignment compromised, and pretty soon it would be back to their cubicles and the salt mines of bureaucratic paperwork and male oppression.

"So, you want to get with the two divorcees?" I asked, watching carefully as Noah feigned his horror. "We'll kill a couple of hours or so, just to blow off tension."

"We don't have time for that," Noah insisted, not bothering to even glance at the two women.

"A couple of hours can't hurt."

He glowered. "Is that all that's on your mind? Pussy?"

"C'mon, just a blow job. You just sit and relax. I'll ask the shorter one if she's good at giving head."

I made like I was about to get up, when Noah grabbed my sleeve. "I said, never mind."

I smiled and sat back down. "Not to worry. Your girls already know their cover's blown."

"How's that?" He played ignorant, refusing again to glance in their direction.

"What's the point of it? You don't trust me? You think I would give you up to Louie?"

"They're here for your protection."

"Yeah. Sure they are."

Noah frowned and clenched his fists. "I don't have to explain anything to you."

"No, you don't. It's obvious. You're worried I'd sell you out."

"It's been done before," he assured me in his all knowing voice. "Money can water down a lot of personal integrity."

"You're really an asshole," I sighed.

"What?!"

There was no need to answer. I just shook my head and walked out of the Café Du Monde. A couple hours later I was on a plane back to LA.

chapter

ELEVEN

I figured Noah would have to call me sooner or later. I didn't believe he was particularly concerned for me, nor did his excesses in New Orleans embarrass him. He would call because he was concerned for himself, for having taken a risk by including me in this odd little stage play only to see me stalk off the set. I had teamed up with a proud man, a suspicious egomaniac from a bygone world. And if my guess was right, he would rather suffer the indignity of my disrespect than the indignity of giving up on his agenda with me.

One morning the telephone rang early. I guessed it was Noah, but I was wrong. Instead, Ray Dannenberg was talking nervously on the phone.

"Where you been, you sonofabitch? I haven't seen you for awhile."

"I've been kind of busy," I said, knowing from the moment I opened my mouth it sounded like bullshit.

"Yeah, well, when are we going to get together again? I thought maybe we would get some dinner."

"Dinner. Yeah. Alright." Even then, I was wondering why in the hell I was accepting his invitation.

"Maybe some time this week?"

"You tell me."

We made plans for later in the week. An hour later, Louie called me. I can't say I was surprised, particularly. As dangerous as it might be, I had to laugh at the way they were trying to work me.

"I'm having dinner with Ray this week."

"Yeah, I know. Ray's a good man. Brilliant. You two could make a helluva team."

"Want to join us?"

"Nah," Louie answered, sounding surprised and flattered. "You two should be alone to get to know each other."

I met Ray Dannenberg at his place in West Los Angeles. His two-bedroom bungalow was sparsely furnished, and the rear yard boasted an ancient redwood hot tub that had split at the seams, rendering it useless. Cheap posters served as wall covering, and the second bedroom had been turned into an office, with shelves on every wall but the sliding closet. Technical books and periodicals filled the bookcases. Judging from the dust, most publications had been shelved for quite awhile. And Ray, in the fading twilight, looked older than I remembered. Wrinkles creased his boyish face, and there were bags under his eyes. It looked like either he had been sleep deprived or drinking too much. I couldn't tell which.

Ray and I ate down in Japan Town in some little hole in the wall Ray had been patronizing for years.

"It's the best sushi in town," he boasted, in what was a now familiar phrase among sushi mavens.

The food was good enough, and Ray was clearly knowledgeable about Japanese Cuisine. While my tastes followed the more conventional salmon, tuna and yellowtail, Ray downed ravenously the squid and the octopus, along with sweet shrimp and some other snotty stuff I didn't dare inquire about. Ray knew the language somewhat, making sure to impress me by ordering and then tossing around a few choice words in Japanese.

"So where have you been hiding yourself?" he asked me. "Louis has been worried you don't keep in touch."

"I talked to Louis earlier today. You're right. I should've called him. One day slips into the next, and before you know it, the week is gone."

"Louis was worried he said something, or maybe did something to you. He's a very sensitive guy."

"He's brutal. All that stuff he does to you between open and spit."

It took Ray a few seconds to realize I was referring to Louis' dentistry. Finally he giggled. "That's funny. You're a good guy. You and I; we could be a powerhouse. I mean that."

"Doing what?"

"Anything we want. After we eat, I want to show you something. You've never seen my place of business."

Ray drove us across town toward El Segundo, where we turned onto a quiet side street filled with modest structures built to accommodate commercial services and light industry. Stopping in the driveway, Ray jumped out and unlocked the chain lock he had wrapped around the cyclone gateway. Like the fencing surrounding the building's perimeter, the twelve foot gate was topped with concertina wire, reflecting off the security lights like angry shark teeth.

The interior of Ray's factory was orderly. Production machinery occupied one section of the floor, and inventory and parts were stocked in another. A few vintage automobiles stood in the corner, including an old Helms Bread Truck, from the bygone era when bakeries delivered house to house. A glass-fronted office occupied much of the rear partition.

"What's it you do again?" I asked looking round.

"Telecom, mainly. I'm working on a few things that could give me a bigger share of the market. Inventions of my own."

"Good for you. The entrepreneur."

"Yeah, just every time I get it on track, something distracts me. If it's not the government on my back taxes, then it's an ex-partner with his bullshit. If it's not that, it's the bigger companies threatening to file lawsuits against patent infringements. I'm telling you, being in business for yourself is a monumental pain in the ass."

"Must be tough, keeping the cash flow," I volunteered as a gesture of sympathy.

"Here," he waved. "Take a look at this."

I followed him through a heavy metal door to a backroom, where various industrial machines stood in even rows. I knew I was supposed to be impressed, but lacking any real mechanical expertise, all I could do was nod and stare.

"Nice. What's this one?" I asked, pointing to a mint green machine.

"Swiss Jig Bore. Can bore metal down to the tolerance of three thousandths of an inch."

"What's it used for?"

He laughed. "Lot of things. For making parts. That one, it cost me a little more than twenty grand. I'll probably turn it for something like eighty."

"No shit?"

"No shit. C'mon," he smiled. "I'll show you something else."

I followed him to the vintage milk truck and watched him duck inside and rattle around for a couple of seconds. He soon emerged, producing a pair of Uzi sub-machine pistols and an old Thompson sub-machinegun, World War Two or Korean surplus.

"I love this," he said, handing me the old Tommy Gun. "Feel the wood, the steel. It's when weapons were carefully machined and not just stamped out on sheet metal."

Hefting the Thompson, I admitted Ray had a point. It was heavy and solid, had the kind of feel that promised never to let you down. Ray was smiling. He looked like a much younger boy, showing off the bicycle he received for Christmas.

"How long have you had this?"

"Since I was a kid. Louis gave it to me."

"You've known him that long, huh?"

"Yeah, we go way back. Louis was a friend of my father."

"Where's your father?"

"He's dead. It's been awhile."

"Sorry."

Ray shrugged. So tell me, how can you and I make some money together?"

"Rob trains. I don't know. I haven't given it much thought. Why? What were you thinking of?"

"I'm not sure. I just figure we would make a pretty good team."

"And Louis?"

"Louis does what Louis does. I do what I do. You see his neighbor much? That guy, Noah?"

Well, talk about a question from out of the blue. "In flurries," I said as casually as possible. "He's been talking to me about writing stories about his exploits during the Second World War. You think that stuff sells anymore?"

"I read it. Sometimes. But, yeah, it sells...to that whole generation."

"He's supposedly one hell of a scientist. Especially in advanced radio frequency imaging and communication. He tells me things, here and there, but most of the time I don't know what in the hell he's talking about."

"Stay close to him. He could make us money."

"That's what Louis said. How is this old man going to make us money?"

"There's a lot to learn from him."

Ray hefted the vintage Thompson and started aiming it at different targets about the warehouse.

"The thing is this," he proposed, squinting behind his glasses. "Power is information, and information leads to wealth. Noah has some valuable information. You're a bright guy. I don't have to tell you that. Noah's a man of pride and principle, but he also likes money. And besides, from what Louis says, he's a lonely guy."

"You want me close to him, right? In case he decides he wants to open up to me."

"No, no. He'll never decide. Not all by himself. To get him to be more forthright, well, you have to use your imagination."

I would have laughed had the situation not been so blood chillingly serious. Ray was outright propositioning that I pimp for him. He may not have expected an answer that night, but I sensed he would want one pretty shortly.

I didn't argue. I was seeing the picture. The boys were getting nervous that Noah, their big fish, was about to snap the line and dive for deep water. I remembered how furious the mysterious Chinese woman had been the night she tore Louie a new asshole for failing to lure Noah to his nephew's party. And now they were placing their hopes in me.

Prevailing worry appeared to be that if I parted company with my new friend Noah, then the bridges would burn, the highways would crumble, and their connection would be lost, maybe forever. I was their way in—since I was closest to Noah, perhaps I could convince him to play some winter ball for the Chinese team. Noah, the same guy I left back in New Orleans.

chapter

TWELVE

I went about my business for almost two weeks, hearing nothing from nobody. I wasn't surprised. Ironically, both sides had decided at the same time that I should sit and stew in my juices. As the days passed, I gave perfunctory thought to Noah and Louis, wondering if they had a clue that I could see right through their tactics. I wondered if it was a generational thing, or if I had just been on the streets long enough to understand they were pretending to abandon me to the ice floe. I was also taken with their inflated sense of self-importance. I'm sure they thought I suffered and worried. Yet while I grew snide about their outmoded foolishness, I also recognized they had gotten to me. Nevertheless, I was determined to tough it out.

Louie was the first to call. "How are you doing?" he asked like a father missing his son off at college. "Have you seen Noah?" he asked, promptly switching his tone of voice.

"No. Can't say I have. Not for awhile."

"You know one day that sonofabitch will push me a little too far." It was as if Louie had shifted gears, and now Louis the Killer was doing the talking.

"I'm telling you, he likes to throw his weight around, says I'm talking out of school. I don't talk about him. I don't blow people's secrets. Hell, I'm a world full of secrets. I've kept so many secrets sometimes I think I'll burst inside. Everyone confides in me. Even Noah."

"He does?"

"Hell, yeah. He told me all that stuff about himself. Then he turns around and blames me. You know how I am about not betraying friendship. I'd just as soon cut your throat then give up your confidences."

"Given the choice, I'd rather have you betray my confidences than cut my throat, Louis."

"Well, you know what I mean."

I didn't, but I decided it wasn't the time to push for a clearer definition.

"You're a good guy, Louis. But sometimes I think you tend to get carried away. As far as you and Noah go, you guys are always going to squabble. It's just the way it is."

"You don't hold nothing against me, do you?" he asked, again changing his persona to the worried, sensitive intellectual he maybe once started out to be.

"Of course not."

I could tell by his breathing, he was calming down. For a schizoid with homicidal tendencies he was pretty sensitive, after all.

"You know I'd never do anything to hurt you," he reassured me.

"Of course I know that. How's Ray?" I asked. I was feeling sorry for Louie and hoping to change the subject.

"He's doing good, working on one of his projects. You guys had dinner together."

"Yeah. Remember, we talked about that? He showed me his place. Great place."

"You stick with Ray. Ray knows how to make big money. And you know, anyone gives you any problems, you talk to either Ray or me. Look, I've got to go now."

And with that he was off the phone. Long before, I discovered that Louis had apparently picked up from his Chinese friends the Asian custom of saying goodbye and then departing right after. Most Americans won't do that at the risk of sounding abrupt or impolite, preferring to lollygag with postscripts and afterthoughts, before their final departure. Asians, generally, say goodbye and they're on their way, off the phone or out the door. Like Louie.

Twelve days later Noah called me. Let's grab an early dinner," he said. "We've got a lot to talk about."

I arrived a few minutes late, parked and started for the entrance to Santo Pietro's when I felt eyes on me. I noticed a couple in their late twenties, early thirties, sitting in the restaurant patio of Le Baguette, a French pastry and salad place. The man appeared to be of Eastern European extraction and the woman was Chinese. They were nursing Cappuccinos and pretending to be engrossed in each other's conversation. As I started for the entrance to Santo Pietro's, she stood and headed toward the phones at the rear of the bakery. Somebody wanted to know when I arrived.

I found Noah at the tiny bar in Santo Pietro's, conversing with an attractive Chinese woman in her mid-to-late thirties. We were by now familiar figures there, and one of the waiters said hello to me. I slowed my pace, noting how the Chinese woman dressed in tailored clothing and carried herself like a professional. I tried to catch a better look at her face off the reflection in one of the mirrors, but to no avail. Catching Noah's eye as he gestured discretely for me to join them, I sidled up to the bar and ordered a glass of wine. There were two glasses of wine already on the counter. One belonged to Noah and the other, still full, belonged presumably to the Chinese woman.

"You're late," Noah announced much to my surprise. I had hardly expected him to acknowledge me, yet alone invite me to participate in their friendly chat.

"This is Cindy," he gestured as an introduction. "Cindy is a marriage counselor, and she lives up in Fresno. We were talking about Stanford, where Cindy went to school. And we were talking about the difference in relationships between the Americans and the traditional Chinese."

"Really? And what about a relationship between an American and someone Chinese?" I smiled. Cindy smiled back at me. She was prettier than I remembered. There was no sense in bullshitting each other. She had recognized me; she just wasn't sure if I recognized her.

"Do people always come to your office, or do you sometimes make house calls?" I asked. "It would make sense if you studied their environment."

She pretended not to understand me at first, but that was all for show. Cindy spoke English with a homegrown American accent.

"I don't make house calls."

"So, what are you doing in town?"

"I'm here to see friends."

"Good friends?" Noah wondered.

"Yes."

"Then they'll understand if you're late. Why don't you join us for dinner?"

I wasn't surprised when she glanced at her watch.

"I can't, really."

"You're sure?"

"Quite." She batted her eyes at Noah. "Maybe some other time."

She snatched her cigarettes from the bar and tossed them into her handbag. Another smile and she hurried out the door.

Noah studied Cindy's still full glass of wine. "I tried to get her prints by ordering her a glass of wine. But she wouldn't bite."

Sighing, he drained the glass and set it down on the bar with a thump.

"So tell me the truth. Does she really have a thing for me? Or is she who I think she is?"

"I hate to burst your bubble, but maybe we should follow her?"

"It's being done as we speak. There are three teams of federal agents working the parking lot."

"Good. Because there's another couple next door. Eastern European guy and a Chinese woman."

"Maybe they're the ones in the old Porsche that's been hanging on my tail."

"Have you noticed; there are a lot of spooky characters around here lately?"

"I attract them like flies."

We sat down at a table. Rather than order a medium pizza like everyone else, Noah formed his short-sleeved arms into a hairy circle to indicate the size of the pizza desired.

"A cheese pizza, this big around," he demonstrated in his now familiar ritual. "And your Lowenbrau on tap."

"Why don't you just order a medium pizza, instead of all the charades?"

"It tastes better this way."

"You missed a helluva trip," he gloated, soon after his pizza and my salad arrived at our table. "I went to maybe three, four cities, and each one has the same set up we found here."

"And that is...?"

"More downed fliers. Korean POW's. They're old men now. Most of them, anymore, are just figureheads. New Orleans has one of the largest and oldest operations. Our boy Shockley was a charter member of the New Orleans group.

"They're all set up just like the Roberts Trust. They front as holding companies for a variety of businesses, mostly in technology. Many of the companies, though small, are ostensibly reputable institutions."

"How did you find this out?"

"Ran the list of Korean POW's. Where are they now? Many of them are dead, and most of the others are retired or off in the usual stuff, doctors, lawyers, business people. And then there were those who met the requisite parameters. Roberts and Tom Raymond, by the way, were prisoners in the same Korean POW camp."

"But why fliers?"

Noah shrugged. "Hard to say. Most of the POW's were enlisted men. The bulk of the officers had to be downed Air Force fliers or Navy Aviators. I'm guessing on this, but the Chinese probably saw them as leadership material. Because many were seriously injured or crippled, they may have been embittered by their wartime experience. Probably there were some who couldn't see how they would make a living, once the war was over. Remember, Korea was not a popular war.

"Most of the officers, the pilots anyway, were kept together. They were sent up to Manchuria, where the Chinese had a crack at them. You take any group and work on them long enough and some will start to see it your way. Especially if there's money in it."

"And Louie. He was supposedly in Air Force Intelligence, but he was never a prisoner of war. I think he said he used to analyze the results of bombing missions."

"I know," said Noah, lighting up a cigarette. "Every now and then we'd send our planes out, and they would get all chewed to hell, as if the Gooks were waiting for us. It could've been the Louie's of the world."

"So we're talking about what? Brainwashing? But what about the Bishop, people like that? We know his background is mostly bogus, but where does he come in?"

"He's originally of German nationality. But instead of being a Stalinist like most red Europeans, he has more of a Maoist bent."

"So you have turncoat Americans and Maoist Europeans assigned to establish legitimate companies so they can develop, buy and then smuggle technology and equipment back to Mainland China. And you're saying it's all been operating under our noses since after the Korean War?"

"Hoover used to warn us about it, the infiltration."

"Well, maybe he got something right."

I could see by the scowl that Noah didn't like that. "Don't believe all that propaganda. J. Edgar was way ahead of the pack."

"And here I thought he was stuck in the closet."

"That's all bullshit. There were women in his life."

"His mother, maybe."

"You believe whatever trash you want to believe."

"Getting back on track here. The Chinese have been infiltrating our system since the early, middle fifties, using disenfranchised Americans, assorted nut jobs and whatever else they could find. That's what you're saying?"

"Don't forget. The nut jobs come in handy when you need someone for the wet work. So far, we can trace seventy-one related murders back to this group. Most of the victims were grand jury witnesses. You use a nut, and you have built in deniability. They start talking conspiracy, and nobody believes them."

I nodded. "The Chinese were desperate. That would be my take. The fifties, sixties and even most of the seventies were still Cold War. It was the era of the Iron Curtain, or the Bamboo Curtain in China's case. We had no trade agreements, and we certainly didn't allow them to immigrate into the States the way we do now.

"So who are you going to get to work for you? Someone successful? I doubt it. The average American Joe, who is happy with our way of life? Hell, no! You get the nut jobs and the foundational losers, the types who believe they are not appreciated for their special talents and inherent qualities. You get Louie."

"You're learning," smiled Noah, a little too condescendingly for my tastes. "That's just about where it's at. At least, that's how it started.

"Like I told you, Louie is mostly a money deal. He was there initially to facilitate espionage and smuggling operations and to prevent discovery of the network. Besides any witnesses, he was also assigned to eliminate competition stemming from the Japanese, Russians, and even the French and Germans who were also competing to steal our technology.

"Like the ones Louie has claimed to have executed?"

"He doesn't work in a vacuum. The 'they' people Louie always talks about but can never really define? His obsession with the storing of weapons, explosives and food, you know what that's all about?"

"He's part squirrel."

"Before Nixon opened up China, there was a better than average chance we would end up in another war with them. In case that war happened, Louie and the boys were assigned to commit sabotage."

"Poison the wells. Assassinate key people. Blow up the infrastructure. Stuff like that?"

"Exactly. If the balloon ever went up, they would start blowing bridges, killing local officials. Whatever."

"Did the Chinese know they were assigning the task to madmen and outcasts?"

Noah flicked ashes from his cigarette. "You were right the first time. Desperation. The Chinese recruited whoever they could. They couldn't afford to be choosy. But things are different now. With all the Chinese Nationals pouring into this country, the rules of the game have changed dramatically."

I shifted in my seat and sipped my iced tea. "How much did Louie earn for selling out his country?"

"As far as we can tell, in excess of a half million in subsidiary earnings. Plus all the goods he could steal."

"You have to admire them, the Chinese. It's a wonderfully intricate structure. It's so well thought out, like a giant puzzle. Talk about a scalable enterprise"

"Like I said, Pearl Harbor to us is ancient history. To the Chinese, planning for one hundred years is nothing. China for one thing has a history of honoring its spies. In the United States we tend to vilify the intelligence community."

"The intricacy is pretty amazing," I marveled.

"Makes the Russians look like a bunch of pig farmers. Their methodology is very different. Where the Russians will cultivate an espionage program, one or two people working on their target, the Chinese will send dozens of people, each making a separate overture. That's why I'm getting so many odd phone calls from all over the place. They are mostly Chinese, judging by their accents, calling me from pay phones and hotel rooms. They want to offer me consulting work in their technology businesses. It's like I'm on the multiple listing service in the Chinese Intelligence Network."

"What's remarkable is they have no sense of consequence."

"Uh huh. But the truly key difference between the Russians and Chinese espionage networks is this. The Russians would have to pay out of pocket through the KGB for their intelligence service and assets. It's a terrible drain on their resources. The Chinese figured out a way to maintain operations through self-sustaining, profit making organizations."

"Plus, with their companies seemingly legitimate and reputable, they have easy access to many components in defense and technology. Really brilliant."

Noah shrugged noncommittally. "Another thing. It took some doing, but I got hold of some of Louie's medical records. Apparently it's true; thirteen years ago he had been ripped off by a couple of swindlers. Those he did kill, along with his receptionist, who served as their accomplice. He was judged too insane to prosecute, but they did manage to have him committed. For five years Louis sat near comatose, just staring at the walls. He spent four at a sanitarium and more than a year at his mother's house.

"It wasn't the first time. Louie is a textbook case, about ninety percent predictable. He can enter a violent maniacal period and lash out at anyone, before lapsing into general catatonia.

"After the last major episode, that's when he really got more deeply involved in this gun thing. I think it was the shrink who encouraged him. The shrink is a regular asshole by the name of Laird Gessner. The lawyer who partially represented Louie during the breakdown is a guy named Barry Storm. Storm is another downed flier, confined to wheelchair. I'm not sure if it was Korea or Vietnam. Storm has a partner—the shrink's son, Albert Gessner.

"It's a family affair. Cozy."

"Storm and Gessner used to pay their secretary in cash. They paid her like that for thirteen years. When she asked to go on payroll, they fired her.

"Albert Gessner. He has a very fishy past. He was part of this veteran's rights group for Korean War Vets. Gessner worked out of California, but there were chapters in different cities. We always thought it was some commie front, but we didn't know how or why it was in operation."

Noah frowned and continued. "Apparently he was part of the legal effort to set up the trusts and establish the original infrastructure. He helped coordinate operations between the downed fliers and the other operatives working here."

"Then they toss in a few front companies, a couple of offshore corporations, and you can buy technology legitimately. And then, by listing a phony end user on your bill of lading, you can ship to countries on the forbidden list. Your friend, Dannenberg, that's part of his operation."

I nodded. "And this has been going on for how long?"

He ignored me. "You know, in the Federal Building we have a bunch of eight foot tables piled maybe five to six feet high with files. It's nearly the end of July, and what we thought was a two month investigation no longer has time restraints. The inter-agency task force has been expanded to over two hundred people. And that isn't nearly enough, not to keep an eye on all the creepy crawlers in all the cities we're looking into."

"Well, I'm sure their hearts are in the right place, but, honestly, a few have their heads up their asses."

I removed papers from an envelope and showed him what I had done. "I did a little homework while you were away. These are all the places where there's a listing for a Old Holy Church. Most are semi-converted houses or commercial lofts. There's a pretty good-sized one in Hollywood, and another in Alhambra, of all places. There are people working there, and living there. Strange characters. I couldn't tell if they were actually tied in with the Bishop, or if they didn't have a clue what he was up to."

Noah looked the papers over, nodding in appreciation. "The boys would have gotten to this, sooner or later."

I shook my head in disgust. "All the information was in the Yellow Pages. Under churches."

Noah just stared like he wanted to kill me, but couldn't justify it no matter how hard he tried.

"Here's another thing. I've been giving thought as to why Louie's so desperate to use me to get to you. Time is running out for them. Like you just said, the Chinese Nationals are moving in on his turf, and Louie knows it. His team needs to score big time to stay in the game."

"Yeah, they want me alright. Apparently there is a wish list of 108 people, all related to the government or the Fortune

1000. I'm on that list. Hell, Louie built me up so big, I'm irresistible."

"The Chinese Nationals are of a different generation. They have no respect for Louie and his past contributions. You could use that rivalry. You could play one side against the other."

Noah stared at me for the longest time. He said nothing. He didn't have to. He knew I was right.

He handed the waitress the check with a generous amount of cash, and he told her to keep it. I pulled back the table to make it easier for him to stand.

Noah stood up, and I joined him as he shuffled out of the patio dining area toward his car. He hadn't taken ten steps when he suddenly froze in his tracks. I watched his mouth open and his body tense, as he revealed for the first time obvious signs of wariness and befuddlement. I had never seen him look so worried as he stared in the direction of an elderly couple frozen on the sidewalk some fifteen yards away. The elderly man Noah was looking at was short and stocky, and he looked like a cross between Nikita Khrushchev and Popeye the Sailor. His female companion looked like a classic Russian Babushka, but one who shopped at Hermes and Celine. She was as grim faced as he was and used to heeding his subtle commands. He could only be her husband. To say they looked out of place in the middle of the Glen Centre made the usual understatement seem like hyperbole. Call Rocky and Bullwinkle—the real Boris and Natasha had come to Beverly Hills.

And now in this tony shopping center, two cold war dinosaurs were squaring off amid a backdrop of fashion and luxury. While unsuspecting shoppers scampered from beauty shop to butcher shop, I watched Noah and Popeye suck it up and walk slowly toward each other, watching for any sudden moves. Clearly, these two were used to playing cat and mouse in a game that had twisted and turned over seven continents for more than forty years. And despite their fears for their own mortality, I sensed they were actually getting off on this lethal dance. As it turned out there were no sudden moves. Noah and I strolled past the elderly couple with little more than a subtle glance. But that glance had said enough.

"What was that all about?" I wanted to know as soon as we were safely out of earshot.

Noah took a deep breath and lit up a cigarette. I could see, despite his steel veneer, he remained somewhat shaken.

"That was General Maxim Savadov, former member of the Soviet-American Institute of Sciences. He's one of the top men in the KGB. He wants to talk to me."

chapter

THIRTEEN

I would soon learn that Savadov's barely perceptible nod was a signal for Noah to call their mutual associate, a woman whom they both trusted. She was a former Major in the KGB who, after devoting much of her life to the Soviet cause, had defected to the United States some ten years earlier. Her name was Eugenia Kofsky.

A day later I sat with Noah in the rear booth of a nondescript old-fashioned roadside eatery that was nestled halfway up the El Cajon pass. The café was part of a vanishing breed of independently owned local food joints that had the word Eats written in neon back in the time when such electrical scrawling was neither post modern nor kitsch. Unlike the many other establishments that had been abandoned to the savagery of restaurant chain expansion, leaving behind only their weathered remains as fodder for termites and nostalgia junkies, this place survived, miraculously. It served mediocre food equally to truckers and tourists. It was the perfect choice for a meeting. It was out of anyone's way, and its picture windows afforded a perfect vantage point to observe anyone approaching or any suspicious activity.

"You sure you can trust this woman?" I asked, wondering if this was not the kind of trap that years later would be a footnote in the history of intelligence services.

"Stop worrying. This is why we keep her, so she will make these kinds of arrangements. She's top notch. You know what kind of accomplishment it is for a woman to be in Division S of the First Directorate?"

"No idea."

"She ran spies, Soviets and Americans, while working out of the UN. And at times her team would perform the occasional wet work."

"But she defected. Why would the Russians trust her?"

As if on cue, a short stocky woman in a gray skirt, white blouse and three-quarter-length leather jacket entered the restaurant, clutching an oversized handbag. She looked neither left nor right, but walked deliberately in a manner that would attract the least attention. When she spotted us, she raised her eyebrows just slightly and made for our booth in easy strides. Despite her pleasant face, which over the years had taken on the character of an aging grandmother, there was no denying either her physical strength or the quiet kind of melancholy that was encased in her being. Her countenance projected the kind of grudging resignation acquired from backing a loser for far too long.

"The meeting is set for tomorrow night," Eugenia Kofsky announced, while sliding a hand written note across the table to Noah. "The address and time," she said.

"He say what it's about?" Noah asked, after glancing over the note and sliding it into his jacket pocket.

"No, but if Savadov came all this way, it has to be important. He's never one for trifles," she assured Noah.

"Funny, but we never picked up on the fact he entered the country."

Kofsky smiled condescendingly. There still remained in her a clinging sense of pride that she was once a part of the KGB. "He came by submarine. Through Washington State. He came down here looking for a friend of yours. When he couldn't find him, he came looking for you."

Eugenia Kofsky lit up a cigarette and smiled at me. It was a cold smile, but probably the friendliest she could hope to manage. She glanced at me in a casual appraisal, perhaps assessing why Noah had me hanging around. She smiled again, but this time her smile was different, a type of acknowledgment or sign of satisfaction.

I nodded back and made no effort to conceal the fact that I was studying her hands. She kept them still for me to look at; her eyes were watching my own. Her hands weren't exactly the most feminine, but they were not particularly masculine, as the cliché would so easily have it. They were mannered hands, and as such they revealed her underlying cultivation. For me, an amateur palm reader, the lines in her palms revealed among other things, intelligence and a touch of morbidity. Big surprise.

"How long were you married?" I asked, letting her know what I saw in her hands.

She was taken aback and tried not to show it. Noah, too, was more than a little surprised.

"I'm a widow," she said. "If you're good enough, you'll figure it out."

"That's why you decided to come here? Your widowhood came unexpectedly."

She nodded, grateful I had not chosen to use the word defection.

"You're a smart boy. Intuitive. No wonder this old man wants you around."

She sighed and turned to Noah. "It's a long way for a cup of coffee."

"I'm careful. You know that."

Kofsky laughed. "Who cares anymore? Our greatest danger is the citizens of our respective countries. They're the ones who hate our kind. Your former adversaries, they share too much in common to want to do you any harm. We're members in a dying club."

A few minutes later Eugenia Kofsky was gone. We followed soon after. I wouldn't see Kofsky again for almost a year. On that occasion she would help weigh the wisdom of liquidating Louie and a few of his friends. She was all for it, and she promised the Americans could keep their hands clean. There were favors owed her, and there were agents in the KGB who would kill them in the name of a better personal relationship with their western counterparts. Like Kofsky had said a year earlier, it was a club, and at this point they shared an understanding they could never communicate to their own citizens. The world is indeed a strange place when your allies and your enemies are often the same.

Noah took me by surprise when he asked me to drive him to his meeting the following night with KBG General Maxim Savadov. The meeting was to be held in a safe house in the Hollywood Hills, overlooking the semi-seedy Hollywood flats where Russian immigrants and more than a few of Savadov's former comrades were beginning to settle. I assumed the Savadov meeting had been turned over to official channels for approval and strategic policy. I assumed executives at the highest levels of intelligence would be made aware of the meeting. I thought for sure I'd be left out in the dark for this one. But Noah, as usual, had other ideas.

"I haven't told anyone about this," Noah explained, "except a couple of my closest associates. If this little sit down becomes official, then someone might turn it over to State or even to the wrong people in my own group, and they might start getting stupid ideas. We don't need the publicity."

"That would be crazy. Even I know that."

"Maybe some glory seeking asshole wants to demonstrate Soviet-American cooperation in the spirit of Glasnost. Someone in desperate need of Brownie points could leak it to the State Department. If it goes public, then the Russians will back off and deny contact was even made, and then we'll never know what they wanted. Whatever value this meeting can offer goes right out the fucking window. Kofsky was right. Savadov didn't come to town just to pull my chain."

"Yeah. But what's with his wife?"

"A symbol. To show he had come in peace."

"It's so old world it's almost quaint."

"It ain't so quaint when you consider it's the KGB you're dealing with. It's more like relief."

Noah sighed, pausing as he usually did when he deliberated about being candid with me. "Look, I know it's a cliché, but the fact is, you're never sure who you can trust in this business.

"Savadov and I go back a long way. He's in the Russian Academy of Sciences, and we shared many years on committees for the exchange of science and technology. If I were to lead him into a cluster fuck, I would lose his confidence forever."

"A strange turnaround, since up at the Glen Centre the other day you were worried he was planning to kill you."

"That was the other day."

I turned up one of the narrow, twisting streets that led up into the Hollywood Hills. Nearing the top, I turned onto an even narrower street that led to a quiet trail, turning to dirt at the end. A rustic one story wood frame house was set on a weedy bluff overlooking the city lights below.

Two Russians dressed in leather jackets and blue jeans were waiting for us in the front. The muscle. As we parked, got out of the car and started toward the front of the house, a more refined middle-aged man in a navy blue suit stepped out from the entrance to greet us.

"Did you find us alright?" he asked in the kind of English he learned after having spent years in America.

"I'm always able to find you," Noah remarked, an unmistakable double entendre that caused the Russian to raise his eyebrows in vintage disdain.

The Russian regarded me with weary suspicion and turned to Noah. "You agreed to meet with the General alone."

"That's right," Noah said, turning to me. "You'd better wait out here."

As Noah went inside, I retreated back to the car and spent the next hour or so listening to the radio and taking in a view of the city lights. It was a clear, moonless night, and it was easy to spot the satellites in orbit, the flashing lights of jet planes traversing the sky. Down below was the city grid, all glitzy and pulsing with neon and the expectations of millions of people who had come to Los Angeles to live out their dreams. I found it so odd that just a thousand feet above them talks were being held in a former Hollywood hideaway that could help decide at least a few events concerning these two major nations.

Restless, I got out of the car and walked to the edge of the property where I could look out over the city. I felt as if I was standing in one world and looking into another, a world I had impulsively left behind. Momentarily, I longed for that world that, despite its hype and fantasy, seemed so straightforward compared to the complexity, deceit and illusion so pervasive in espionage and international struggle.

That desire to return soon faded. I wasn't fooling anyone, especially myself. I liked my new world; I was stuck now, drawn to its game like a moth to the flame.

I heard a rustle and footsteps crunching toward me. I stiffened as I turned to face the two Russians who were approaching. Here it comes I thought, in that first flash of paranoia. For the briefest instant I thought I was trapped, and I was about to take a header into the world only seconds ago I had longed for. I relaxed somewhat when I saw no threatening gestures in their body language.

"Hey," the balding one said in a thick Russian accent. "Maybe you could tell us something."

"Depends what you're asking."

"Do you go to nightclubs?"

What a question, given the circumstances. Twenty yards away international powers were swapping favors that were moving the world around, and here we were exchanging dancing steps.

"Sometimes."

"Which is your favorite for dancing?"

"Power Tools. It's in the old hotel across from Macarthur Park. It's a major scene."

"Power Tools? That's a funny name for a nightclub. Very proletarian," he laughed.

"Yeah? If you think that's funny, you should see what goes on there."

They laughed again. I tried to picture two agents of perhaps the most feared organization in the world, cruising for a good time among the Goths, the Punks, the transvestites, and the assorted lounge lizards, fetishists and perverts who made these laser ridden spectacles their home.

Our randy attempt at hands across the water was abruptly interrupted when Noah, Savadov, and the woman I had seen in the window appeared in the darkened house entrance. The man in the navy blue suit soon joined them, and the group exchanged parting words and shook hands all around. As the woman and the man in the navy suit stepped back inside the house, Noah took Savadov aside, and they talked softly in the shadows for several minutes. The two men were engrossed in their conversation. I realized this was their sealing the deal, exchanging assurances for whatever transpired inside the safe house. This was each man giving his word of honor, based on their forty-odd year relationship. The others inside the house were merely window dressing, living conduits of messages and policy. If not the ringmasters, then Noah and Savadov were the lion tamers of the circus.

Noah emerged from the shadows, limping toward the car. He was silent, but his eyes were telling me this meeting had great significance. I could read his expressions pretty well by now, especially when he wished it. I held the door and waited for him to get inside the car. It was always an effort—careful squatting, and then, when he had his behind on the seat, he would turn his legs inside the vehicle. After nodding goodbye to the two Russians in leather jackets, I started the car and drove off down the narrow trail. Noah didn't say anything until we reached Sunset Boulevard.

"Like Kofsky said, Savadov did come in by submarine," he began. "He's here because the Russians are very concerned about Chinese espionage operations within the United States. Among other things, they fear the Chinese will steal enough advanced technology to eventually gain a weapons advantage over the Russians."

"I suppose with Glasnost and Perestroika all the rage, the Russians want to get on our good side. Throw the Americans a bone."

"They are sending a defector—a KGB agent. It's a setup from start to finish. We'll debrief him, allegedly to root out American moles that are working for the Russians. But really, he'll be outlining what information they know about Chinese operations within our borders."

"And learning what we know. Do you take them at their word?"

Noah smiled in appreciation of my suspicions. "I trust Savadov only up to a point."

"He looks like Popeye. How much can you trust a guy that looks like fucking Popeye?"

"The thing about the Russians, there's almost always another angle. They can't help it; it's in their nature to augment the truth with disinformation. The minute they lay all their cards on the table, you'd better start checking their sleeves."

"Okay. First off, how do they even know you're investigating Chinese operations within the American borders? It's not public. It's not on CNN. To me, it's one of two ways. They have either committed a lot of KGB assets to tracking your best efforts. Or... they've got a mole working inside the American government. Someone who knows Chinese spies are a high priority."

I enjoyed watching Noah's face flush in recognition of this very distinct yet horrifying possibility.

"There are rumors," Noah grudgingly admitted. "We've never found one. Yet."

"C'mon, you're the one, not me, who goes on about diminishing morality and ethics. Just because it hasn't happened yet, or more accurately, you haven't caught anyone at it yet, doesn't mean some disenchanted scumbag doesn't view the final days of the Cold War as his last chance to cash in on the gravy train."

Noah pressed his lips together, concerned. "That's also why I wanted time, before I presented this formally. If there is a mole, there's no sense in tipping him off."

"Another thing. I haven't said anything to you, but that woman, Cindy, the one you spotted over Louie's house that night?"

"The one who tried to hit on you?"

Noah smiled, flattered and grateful for my fib. "We've been tailing her, and that's been yielding some awfully interesting information. Her real name is Li Chen, and according to her file, she's lived in Los Angeles, Laguna Beach, San Luis Obispo and now Seattle. Not Fresno."

"Girl sure gets around."

"She still commutes from one city to another. But here's the fun part...we believe she has the equivalent rank of Major or Colonel in the Ministry of State Security. From what we can tell, the MSS was just formed a couple of years ago. It's either supplanted some of the other espionage services, or it is in addition to them.

"You did real good with finding Cindy." Noah hesitated, almost choking on the flattery.

"Thanks, but that one was a total accident."

"Some of the best discoveries are accidental. I'll be out of town, during the next few months. When I'm gone, I want you to keep away from Louie and the boys. You never know what's on their minds."

A week later, during the first week in August, as Noah and I sat over morning coffee, CNN announced that Vitaly Yurchenko, a high ranking officer in the KGB's First Directorate, entered the American Embassy in Lisbon, Portugal, and announced he was defecting. The Soviets dutifully put up a ruckus and demanded their KGB Colonel be remanded to their authority. Officials in the State Department, just as dutifully, refused. Days later Yurchenko was brought back to the United States for extended debriefing. The information he would ultimately provide to the Americans and his eventual re-defection would be the subject of controversy for years to come.

Years later, the CIA officer responsible for Yurchenko's debriefing, Aldrich Ames, would prove to be a traitor himself, and one of the highest-ranking moles ever uncovered by American intelligence. Robert Hansen, who was one of the key personnel representing the FBI during the debriefing, would also be convicted of spying for the Russians. With the advantage of hindsight, some today believe it was a premeditated Russian setup from start to finish. As these things often go, it is truly hard to say.

Some believe the Russians sent Yurchenko to take the heat off of Ames, who at the time was under investigation. Ames looked good as the debriefing agent and suspicions were turned to others. Yurchenko gave up a couple of burnt out Russian moles, Edward Lee Howard and Ronald Pelton. He also provided credible information about the Chinese as well. It's a tough call as to what really went down. Like so many other conspiracies, you can often look at it from any angle, and still they all will make sense.

chapter

FOURTEEN

The week of the Yurchenko defection, Noah Brown took off for Washington, D.C., and parts unknown. Sometime after midnight, with the airline terminals nearly empty, I dropped him off in a remote section of Los Angeles International Airport where he would be picked up and flown by government jet to the Capitol. I didn't hear from him for nearly six weeks, until early one morning he called and said he wanted to see me at his house. I found him sitting on his porch, assembling three quarter inch copper metal tubes into what would ultimately be a fifty-foot HAM radio tower.

Like an artisan craftsman out of his time, he patiently picked through the pile of steel and copper piping, aligning each piece and bolting it the main frame. To look at him, you would think he didn't have a care in the world. The radio tower wasn't particularly beautiful; it would never be mistaken for a modern sculpture. Neither the neighbors nor property values would appreciate at the sight of one more skeletal steel contraption rising toward the heavens. But Noah didn't care. For Noah it was often a matter of function over form.

"What's doing?" I asked.

"I've been off conferring with field operations officers in the cities where we've uncovered established espionage networks. Along with the usual configuration, a trust or holding company overseeing the operations of anywhere from four to a dozen different companies, we've also been finding illicit operations we've determined are an immediate threat to the American public. Any immediate threat is given priority and must be eliminated."

"What do you perceive as immediately threatening?"

He set down his pliers and picked up his coffee. He took a thoughtful sip before he answered. I looked around, observing the red and orange leaves falling from the deciduous trees, covering the rusting satellite dish that lay at the bottom of the empty swimming pool.

"You know this whole business about importing assault rifles, AK-47's and the like? They're not being imported from anywhere. They're being made right here in the states. They're making weapons, ammunition and even explosives. We found one such arms production plant in Phoenix, Arizona, and we are looking into others. Some of the guys were over meeting with Louie, and a few headed east toward Phoenix with some of our cowboys hot on the trail. Man, were they pissed off. The cowboys weren't expecting to go on any long trips, and once they had the stooges under surveillance, they couldn't stop to pee or eat for the entire eight-hour drive.

"Anyway, they followed the bad guys back to this old farming machinery distributor and supply shop that has been around for years. It's just outside the city, off a two-lane highway. The supply shop probably was once a legitimate operation.

"All things considered," I started, "I don't find it surprising that the gun nuts are making weapons. It's good business, really."

"It's more than that. Remember, part of their mission is to undermine our national security. By providing weapons to street gangs, dissidents and what have you, they are able to seed unrest and spread violence. You know your buddy, Dannenberg, with his electronics manufacturing facility?"

I nodded.

"We believe he supplements his business by making weapons parts. We've been following their trucks, and Dannenberg is on the route. The trucks pick up from all twenty-two companies in the Roberts Trust. They pick up manufactured gun parts, and sometimes they load the machinery they buy on freighters bound for the PRC. They are all provided with false bills of lading and phony end users. Sometimes they deliver to a clearinghouse, and then the goods are shipped to Phoenix and other cities, or out of the country."

Noah took another sip of coffee and examined the copper tubing on the antenna he was building.

"I need you to do me a favor. I want you to set it up so I can take Louie to lunch."

I stared suspiciously, not saying anything.

"Don't read into it," Noah reassured me. "I just want to take him to lunch. The three of us."

"Lunch?"

"I'm not going to kill him. I mean it."

I shrugged, as if I didn't care either way. I did care. I just wasn't sure why but I retained an odd affection for Louie. I knew I always would..

"Another thing. There's this plastic surgeon, a supposed longtime buddy of Louie's. I think he's been up to no good. I want you to help me break into his office."

"That's illegal," I smiled. "I thought your job was to uphold the law."

"It is. Sometimes that means taking proactive measures."

"Can't you get a warrant?"

"At this point it wouldn't be prudent."

I remembered reading and hearing about higher level agents maintaining their own private assets, keeping things secret from official channels. Like secret little covens, it was said they had their own technicians, people ready to pull black bag operations and even wet work. Although some had been caught and their operations exposed to the public eye, I had still assumed the practice was more apocryphal than real. But then I hadn't met Noah.

I had learned long before this moment that Noah was fond of bypassing sticky red tape and occasionally placing himself above the law. From bits of previous conversations, I had discovered over time that Noah tapped phone lines and bugged houses illegally whenever his intuition commanded. In all, he was one of those old school spooks who viewed the laws that governed his practice as obstacles to be ignored or circumvented. I think with his skills and the necessary equipment the temptation was simply too hard to resist. Until now, I had never passed judgment and, frankly, had never wanted to.

I could foresee certain occasions where such behavior made perfect sense and, arguably, could even be viewed as the moral prerogative. But now here we were at the fork in the road. It was no longer a case of passing judgment, but of going along for the ride.

I had broken laws before. Only now, ironically, I was breaking them for God and country. I saw in that instant where a young, naive and overly patriotic sort could suddenly become very disillusioned. Fortunately, I wasn't one of those. I accepted the fact that my youthful innocence had long departed and had been replaced with the recognition acquired from exposure and experience. Too much exposure, maybe, but there was no way to replay the hand that fate had dealt me. Such is life.

"Here, be useful and hold this," Noah grunted, handing me a socket wrench. "You know about the Freedom of Information Act?"

"Of course. By law it gives American citizens access to a variety of government documents. Including their personal files."

"It also gives every screwball the right to go prowling after confidential documents. Even if some of the material is black lined for security purposes, the better trained can glean enough from what content remains to put two and two together. They can figure out what we're up to, what operations are current and possibly who was involved, how and where."

"Like why the government has been spying on innocent people over the years."

"Innocent is a relative term," he corrected, almost paternally.

"Not when some paranoid asshole views you as a threat and puts you on the shit list for all eternity."

He shrugged. He had heard it before.

"Some like to give sob stories, expressing their buyer's remorse, trying to wring out a little sympathy from the media. The fact is most of them are guilty as hell. Alger Hiss. The Rosenbergs. But that's spilt milk, and not worth getting into. This is today, a genuine threat to our national security. You can see for yourself that these assholes are all over the place."

I shook my head, admiringly. "I love how you spin it. Any minute now you'll be whipping out the flag."

Noah shrugged it off and tried another tack. "Let me put it like this. I've already made up my mind. So don't try to confuse me with the facts. If this is some kind of moral dilemma for you, then let me know now.

I nodded, marveling how my misgivings suddenly paled in the face of what Noah called the bigger picture. The specter of dedicated federal agents getting killed suddenly rested on my shoulders. I would get bad marks on my karmic chart, and that would be tough to live with. I knew intellectually that my involvement was far removed and practically irrelevant. But Noah had his special way of making the morally ambiguous seem almost like a noble pursuit.

I caught him watching me out of the corner of his eye. Noah had amazing peripheral vision. I sensed he and I had played this game before, at other times in different places, over the ages. Speaking of karma, maybe this once again was our cosmic reunion. Still, I was annoyed he knew he was winning on points.

"Part of keeping it confidential means creating as little a paper trail as possible," he said as if the rationale was so simple one had to be a fool to stumble over the nodules of legal irregularity.

"And that means that sometimes we work off the books," he went on. "We get outsiders to handle the black bag operations."

"That's me, the outsider."

He smiled condescendingly. "That's one of the reasons I brought you along for the ride. I thought you'd enjoy all the fun stuff."

He gestured, and I handed him his screwdriver. "I can't deny I'm in it partly for the rush."

"We go in and plant our bugging devices. Listen for a couple of weeks. If there's anything suspicious, anything incriminating, we go get a warrant to legally bug the place."

"Do you pull the original equipment?"

"Sometimes. Sometimes we leave it in place. You're not afraid, are you?" There was that unmistakable challenge in his voice.

I shook my head, no. "So, by my working off the books, this operation never existed. If it didn't exist, there isn't any paperwork that can be discovered through the Freedom of Information Act. I get that part. But aren't you concerned for yourself?"

"I have so many rain checks owed to me, that I'm nearly untouchable," he announced. "Hell, I've been setting up these kinds of operations since before you were born. In the good old days, you could get away with it a lot easier. Especially the wet work. But now you have to finesse it a little more."

"You realize, these aren't the good old days?"

He smiled, inhaling his cigarette. "They weren't then, either."

chapter

FIFTEEN

A few nights later we were making our way in the old beige El Camino, half car and half pickup truck, with its Spartan interior and big assed, rumbling engine. The sound of that engine brought you back to the time when power was measured in cubic inches and not liters or cubic centimeters. A CB antenna protruded through a rusting hole Noah had drilled in the roof of the cab. Noah's burglary and bugging equipment was stashed in the lock box secured on the truck bed. Noah had a gun stashed under the seat. I didn't bring a gun this night, believing that if something went wrong, I had a better chance of talking my way out of it. Best if I wasn't armed while committing burglary.

We parked behind a chintzy single story medical arts building on a corner in the quasi-industrial section of West LA. The building and the main office belonged to a Dr. Victor Burgher, a relatively obscure plastic surgeon. From the looks of the office and the neighborhood, the upscale part of the doctor's practice included C and D Hollywood wannabes who sought tattoo removal, breast augmentation or collagen injections, with a smattering of nose jobs and liposuction thrown in for good measure. The rest of Dr. Burgher's patients were largely clerical and factory workers who may have had real need for reconstructive surgery. But their cheap shit insurance policies demanded they go with third-rate methods. Dr. Burgher had managed to turn his smarmy practice into a lucrative volume business.

We approached the rear entrance to the building and found a solid metal door facing the backside of a body shop and a bakery outlet specializing in day old goods. Removing a spring-loaded lock pick that he noted was good for the "lighter stuff," Noah went to work on the thick steel lock. He worked with the same casual air he showed while building the radio antennas. After a few good squeezes on the pick, he had the lock undone. He put the pick away and turned to me, handing me a piece of paper.

"Here, this should be the alarm code."

"What do you mean, 'should be'? How'd you get the numbers?"

"I took them off his phone lines. When I push open this door, you punch in the code. Ready?"

I nodded and slipped on my white rubber gloves. Noah pushed open the door, and the office alarm started beeping steadily, issuing its warning that in a few seconds the in-office sirens would start blasting and a telephone call would automatically go out to the police. With my heart racing, I ducked inside the office and quickly punched the numbers into the keypad. The beeping stopped abruptly.

"See? Nothing to it."

We switched on smaller sized flashlights and made our way to the steel double layered filing racks located just behind the reception area. The fifteen foot filing racks were typical medical office variety, constructed on runners so you could access the innermost shelf of files by shifting the outer rack to the side. Each rack ran from floor to ceiling and was crammed with thousands of color-coded files. In all, the proliferation of files was an indication of a long and lucrative practice.

Noah handed me a slip of paper, containing a list of file numbers. He also handed me a mini-camera.

"It's cute."

"It is state-of-the-art. Ultra high-speed film for taking pictures in the total darkness. So mind where you shine your flashlight when using the camera.

"The files we're looking for are coded either LD one through thirty four or maybe the initials VB attached to some numerical scale. What you're looking for, if they're dated, should be from the late fifties to the early, maybe middle sixties."

"And you?"

"I need to do a little work on his computer," he winked.

I nodded as I watched Noah drag his black suitcase over to the bookkeeper's desk. In no time he was booted up and running."

I worked by the light of my mini-MAG, moving methodically through the files with the oldest dates on the cover. At first I froze with the flash of each passing pair of headlights, the creaks in the building or noises outside. I soon grew used to the noises and the flashing headlights, although I realized getting caught posed an even greater consequence than only being charged with criminal burglary. In fact, burglary may have been the least of it. The real consequence would come from Louie and the boys, who would realize Noah was onto them.

Ten minutes later I came across my first file on Noah's list. LD-3. I opened the cover and was startled by the before and after photos of a Chinese man in his early thirties. Actually, it was before and after punctuated by a series of photos and X-Rays marking the progressions in between. Some of the pictures were rather repulsive, illustrating the man in a disfigured state with incisions along the cheekbone, the eyes, and the chin.

I figured that was part of the ongoing study, the how-to for future cases of racial transformation. That's what it was, after all, a new racial identity. In the before photo the man was unmistakably Chinese. In the after photo, meaning after the extensive plastic surgery, he had his eyes done, his chin extended, his cheekbones shaved, his brow narrowed; in the after photo the man could pass for European descent.

"This is something else," I whispered to Noah while snapping photos of the file.

"You got them?" He craned his neck for a look-see. "Just keep taking those pictures."

I did. In all, I found fifteen different files, featuring Chinese men of childbearing years undergoing radical transformation. Through the skills of a scalpel wielding, money hungry compadre in West LA, these fifteen Chinese men were not only transported, but also transformed into natives of a different continent. The photos and X-Rays of faces in transition had an eerie, haunting effect on me, and I was feeling again like I had been captured in a horror movie scenario or the back side of the freak show.

I almost didn't hear the car pull up to the back of the office.

"Company," I whispered, closing the file and ducking behind the counter.

I heard a car door slam and realized it was the Rent-a-Cop making his routine inspection. At least I hoped it was his routine inspection, and not something more specific like a tripped alarm. I flattened myself against the floor and out of the corner of my eye I watched the powerful flashlight beam sweeping back and forth across the office. I knew if he spotted something suspicious the Rent-a-Cop would call for backup before he dared enter the office.

I heard the face of the flashlight tapping lightly on the office window as the Rent-a-Cop moved it around for a better view. Abruptly, the sweeping stopped and the flashlight beam remained focused on a darkened corner of the office, just a foot from where Noah was crouching under a desk. And then, just as abruptly, the room went dark again as the Rent-a-Copy flicked off his flashlight and returned to his car. I didn't move until I heard him drive away.

Not long after, Noah and I packed up and took our leave. We were soon at Noah's house, where Noah confirmed I had been looking at the hard, cold evidence of the early and systematic infiltration of Chinese Nationals. I marveled at the dedication of this ancient, yet fledgling nation. I saw in their Cold War strategy the kind of willfulness defining the most sinister aspects of philosophical devotion. For only the most politically devoted or socially desperate would agree to undergo that kind of transition. As a consequence, they would risk losing sense of self and ethnic points of reference.

Noah also showed me several examples of Louie's work. While Noah pissed over the edge of his property and into Deep Canyon, I held x-rays up to the porch light. The dental work wasn't nearly as sensational as the plastic surgery, but the before and after contrasts were impressive.

"It's something, a guy willing to go through all that, just to change his face."

"So they could live here and blend in with the enemy. They would marry only occidentals and sire European-looking children, who through years of dogma would dedicate themselves to the National cause."

"That can backfire," I remarked. "Looking like Europeans they have to lose much of their cultural identity over time. They live among strangers long enough, and they become strangers to themselves."

"That's hardly the point, is it?"

I had to agree. "No, that's hardly the point. So where does Louie come in? He did the dental work, right?"

"Give the man a big cigar. Louie performed the dental work, and then sent them over to our new friend Dr. Burgher for the plastic surgery. Having bugged his phone lines, and his computer, it is clear Dr. Burgher is not the true believer he used to be. Still, he may be someone to pressure, somewhere down the road. If we lean on him, he could be a decent source of information."

"Remember I told you how Louie wanted me to schedule eight hour dental sessions? Like it was no big deal to sit in a dentist's chair for that much time. He and Burgher, they were probably used to it."

"In the good old days, they probably worked twelve and fourteen hours at a stretch. The Chinese Nationals didn't have the luxury of dragging it out. They were all illegal, and they could be caught at any time. And if they were caught, Louie was caught with them.

"Remember, Divinity House, the Bishop's pride and joy, the supposed home for orphaned boys? I think Divinity House had a two-fold purpose. The main reason for the House was so the Bishop could harbor Caucasian or mixed blooded kids brought over from China. The first of these kids came over some years after the Second World War. They posed as Jewish refugees. I don't believe they were Jews. I believe they were German with their legacy really going back to the late nineteenth century when the German based Krupp Industries was selling modern cannons to China.

"Krupp had wanted to save construction and shipping costs, so it built villages where it could house its personnel and build their cannons on-site. I think the Chinese kept the villages pretty isolated, so even the offspring retained their Caucasian features throughout the generations. I think Ray Dannenberg may be one of those kids."

I sat in silence for a moment, picturing how a few more pieces of the jigsaw puzzle were slipping into place.

"But what's this have to do with Louie, or the second reason?"

"For years Louie's old office was right next door to Divinity House. I think they used the orphanage as a safe house. Burgher did his work, and then Louie did his. The Chinese nationals hid out in Divinity House until they recovered from all the surgery.

"Sometimes we tend to underestimate our friend, Louie," Noah said. "We see him now older and debilitated mentally and physically, and we don't stop to realize what a sharp character he was in his prime."

"You mean in between bouts of catatonic psychosis."

Noah tried not to laugh. "He is still a hell of a salesman when he wants to be. I can only imagine how he worked those gun shows and those survivalist conclaves, searching for new blood. He would find misfits and give them religion. Tell them how the country no longer recognized the virtues of the rugged individualist, and then he would assure them that they were not alone. There were others, just like themselves. They were friends of Louie's. Look how he went to work on you."

"I'd say he won a few free games in his time."

"It's that mouth that's the double edge sword. He can use it and be very persuasive, and he can use it to dig his own grave. Which brings to mind the other favor I had asked of you. That is, if you're still willing."

"Louie?"

"Remember when we stopped in Ft. Irwin?"

"On the way back from Las Vegas. Sure. Why?"

"You remember what you saw?"

I remembered. Fort Irwin was the home of the Eleventh Armored Cavalry Regiment. Set approximately halfway between Las Vegas and Los Angeles, many of the mountains inside the base had been hollowed out to store much of the Army's western allotment of ordnance and munitions. The base, itself, was the size of Rhode Island and the only place the Army could conduct full scale desert war games.

But what was particularly significant about Ft. Irwin was the long line of tanks and armored personnel carriers that were mounted on flat cars. Those going inside the base were painted in desert camouflage. Those on the railroad flatcars leaving the base were painted a nice new jungle green.

"I told you where those tanks are going," Noah reminded me. They are being shipped off to Honduras. Just in case the Sandinistas need some real convincing."

"Nicaragua."

"Damn right, Nicaragua. They've been getting equipment from the Soviet Union. Heavy and light tanks, armored personnel carriers, heavy cannon and rocket launchers, as well as your usual mix of Ak-47's. What you saw up at Ft. Irwin was our means of discouraging them from any big ideas."

"So what does this have to do with having lunch with Louie?" I asked. And then the answer came to me. "This had something to do with Bishop and his hard-on for the Sandinistas."

"Every day, every couple of hours, a spy plane flies overhead and keeps watch on the Sandinista buildup. They have been expanding their airstrips in the hopes of receiving advanced fighter aircraft from either the French or the Soviet Union. We have warned them that if one fighter ever lands in Nicaragua, we will retaliate with...well...what you saw. You know why, don't you?"

I knew the answer. He had told me enough times. "Because eventually we will need to build a new canal, and Nicaragua, geographically, is the only place to build one."

"And that is why everyone is fighting over Nicaragua. It's not for principle or ideology, it's for eventual control of a new canal."

"So what's all this have to do with Louie?" I persisted.

"For once I'd like to use Louie's big mouth to my own advantage."

chapter

SIXTEEN

The morning I was to call Louie I read in the Los Angeles Times that there had been a shootout in a Phoenix motel and that a fugitive from justice had been killed along with the first female federal agent to die in the line of duty. The news story claimed that other federal agents had mistaken her for the fugitive's accomplice and had shot her dead.

There was no mention of illegal munitions or weapons factory. In fact, there was little elaboration at all. I knew right away the story was just a cover for a much more significant shootout and the destruction of an illegal munitions factory Noah had mentioned several weeks before. Thanks to Noah, I had learned to read between the lines of most serious news stories. In this particular case, I realized the official explanation was just another piece of Noah's fiction.

I put Phoenix out of my mind and called Louie. I told him that Noah had invited him to lunch. After an alarming moment of silence, Louie responded. I could sense the tension swelling inside him. He was suspicious and filling up with deadly paranoia.

"What for?" Louie asked through grinding teeth.

"Louie, Noah wanted me to assure you he doesn't mean you harm. He wants to show you something, something he believes may be of special interest to you."

"Will you be there?" he asked, sounding a tad child-like in that high, adenoidal register of his.

"Louis, you told me to work him, so I'm working him. Like I said, I wouldn't let him harm you. If anything, this may do you some good."

"What is it?"

"Can't say. I'm not entirely certain myself. One thing though, and this Noah made awfully clear to me. You carry a piece and all bets are off."

The 94th Aero Squadron Restaurant was uniquely designed as a French farmhouse that had been occupied by Allied Forces during the First World War. The first impression upon entering the restaurant was sepia like representation of a war that always seemed distant and without much controversy to my generation. War memorabilia, from helmets to headlines, hung everywhere, and sandbags were piled around the exterior, interlaced with barbed wire and other accoutrements from the War to End All Wars. There were sections of the exterior walls where the white plaster was made to look like Hun canon fire had torn into the brick underneath. All in the bloody landscape known as Van Nuys.

The 94th Aero Squadron also boasted of a full-length picture window that looked out over Van Nuys Airport. Van Nuys Airport was not a commercial airfield, so it played host mostly to corporate jets, private planes and a couple of freighting transports. A runway was positioned just in front of the 94th Aero Squadron, and on Sundays, while stuffing himself on the restaurant's plentiful Sunday brunch, the happy diner could observe pilot owners of vintage aircraft taking off and landing. The sector reserved for the military—hangars, planes and assorted vehicles, loomed across the field.

We no sooner sat at the booth by the window than Noah wasted no time in launching his disinformation campaign. He gestured across the airfield to the military hangars in the distance.

"Louie, don't be obvious about this, but you see across the field, where the military hangars are located?"

Louie started to turn his head, but was quickly admonished by Noah.

"I told you not to be obvious!"

Louie moved in almost slow motion until his eyes focused on the spot where Noah had gestured.

"Yeah?"

"See those planes, taking off and landing?"

"Yeah?"

"Those are C-130 Army Transports. See how one no sooner takes off than another lands?"

"Yeah," Louie answered, only a little more dubiously.

"Do you see it or not?"

"Yeah, I do," agreed Louie.

"They're being loaded up with military supplies," Noah told him. "See how they are all painted a nice new shiny jungle green."

Louie nodded this time, staring silently toward the hangars. Trucks and troops were moving about in front of the mouth of the hangar. As if on cue, a large green C-130 transport taxied over to the runway and took off. Two more stood just off the runway.

"Guess where they are headed?"

Louie wasn't sure.

"The Honduras," Noah prompted. "It's High Noon in Nicaragua."

Louie stared in pensive silence until "Jesus Christ" slipped out from his lips.

"Now look, I don't want you going off with diarrhea of the mouth. I only told you because I know how important Nicaragua is to your friend, Monsignor Kroll."

"May I tell him?"

"Yes, you can tell him. But, otherwise, Louie, I want you to keep it to yourself."

"What kind of forces are we using?" Louie wanted to know.

"It's an invasion. What kind of forces do you think we would use?"

Louie sucked in more air than his lungs were used to holding. He looked down at his ample salad and back out the window, deciding what to ask next.

"Are we going to occupy Nicaragua?"

"Louie, please keep your voice down. I've already showed you enough. You see what you see out the window, don't you? You're a former military man. You were Air Force Intelligence, no less. You can fill in the pieces. What more do you want me to say?"

"But anyone could see them out there."

"Louie, what did I just tell you?"

Louie held up his hands in silent apology. The wheels in his mind, which had been moribund with fear and confusion, were now beginning to turn with blinding speed. He was planning, conniving, and probably elaborating on what he saw before him. An hour after lunch, the story would take on epic form.

Noah and I deliberately reverted to small talk, leaving Louie to stew in his juices.

"How do you like your salad, Louis?" I asked, receiving in return a blank stare and eventual mumbling.

"It's good. But I'm much too excited to eat."

"There's a first," Noah joked. "You're turning down a free lunch."

Louie laughed his grunting laugh. "When is it scheduled? The invasion?"

"Hard to say," answered Noah, building his case for plausible deniability. "All they have to do is give us one good reason to go in. You know them better than any of us, Louie. How long before the Sandinistas give us a reason to kick their ass?"

Another laugh. "If you put it that way, then it could be any day now," Louie mused. "Wait until I tell Kroll."

"Maybe we should all go down there," offered Noah. "It's one thing if you say it. It's another if I tell him."

Louie considered the offer in silence and nodded in agreement. "That would go a long way to boost my credibility," he said.

An hour later we were pulling up to an old Craftsman style house on one of the side streets near the University of Southern California. The once handsome house was in need of a facelift; the paint was faded and peeling and there were signs of dry rot around the windows and under the eaves of the porch. The old screen door needed replacing, and there were planks warping in the dusty porch floor.

A sign informed all who entered that this was a branch of the Old Holy Church—holy ground. The Bishop, dressed in a yellow polo shirt and chinos, was standing in the doorway waiting to greet us. He smiled faintly, but his attempt at cordiality did little to conceal what I took for his survivor's instincts. Clearly he was wary of Noah, and he was suspicious of me. Anyone with any sense knew Louie could be a fuck up, and the Bishop's curiosity and suspicions competed for his attention as he tried to factor in the unknown elements of the dilemma he now confronted.

"I should feel honored," he said. "So many visitors."

"Monsignor," said Noah, offering his hand. "It's a pleasure to see you."

The Bishop took his hand and shook it weakly. "It has been awhile."

The floor in the study was covered with a deep red carpet, and all the walls were lined with books. A simple cross was hanging on the wall opposite the fireplace. There was an old sofa and a matching pair of threadbare chairs, and the kind of dark mahogany coffee table that once belonged to someone's grandmother. We all sat around that coffee table while the Bishop served tea and the type of sugar cookies you buy in tins of three at the Dollar Store.

Sitting on the floor with his legs crossed, the Bishop sipped tea delicately and got right to the point.

"Louis claims you have good news for me."

"They're invading Nicaragua," Louis piped in.

"Louis likes to exaggerate by at least ten thousand times," Noah rushed to explain.

The Bishop smiled thinly. "Louis is known for that."

"American troops are poised and ready. Tanks, armored personnel carriers and other major equipment are being shipped as we speak, and our war planes have been moved into position."

"Why then, if the Americans aren't going to invade?"

"Now, now," admonished Noah. "I didn't say we weren't going to, either. I just want you to realize that it's not one hundred percent absolute."

"What percent is it then?"

Noah pretended to think it over. "Maybe eighty, ninety percent."

The Bishop looked pleased, and he turned and smiled approvingly at Louis.

"Look at it this way," Noah explained with a great pretense of candor. "We've challenged them. We've told them that if a single Russian fighter plane lands on their bases, it will mean a war. But to expand their opportunities in South American, they will need those fighters. They have to challenge us. If not, they will lose all momentum. Without advanced jet fighters, their revolution may never recover."

"So you believe it is really happening?" the Bishop asked of Noah.

"Any time now. That's my gut."

We spent another hour at the Bishop's house, making small talk and listening to the Bishop rant in gentle voice about his evil enemy, the Sandinistas. Now and then the Bishop would probe Noah for additional facts, some of which seemed inconsequential, but all in the room had long recognized the devil was in the details. We left, shaking hands and politely bidding the Bishop goodbye.

"Should I remain behind?" Louie wondered as we made for the door.

"No, Louis," the Bishop replied. "You go with them."

When we dropped Louie off at his driveway, he couldn't conceal his impatience as he fumbled with the keys to unlock the gate. He all but ran to his house.

"Either he has to take a mighty shit, or there are some serious phone calls to make," I quipped.

"In minutes he'll be lighting up the phone lines," Noah acknowledged.

After we parked at his house and got out of the car, Noah pulled out a second key chain, the one that sported a plain brass medallion about the size of a half dollar.

"You noticed how carefully the Bishop held his cup while drinking his tea?"

He demonstrated, spreading his thumb and first finger. "Just like that, so he could hold the cup between his thumb and his finger, never letting his finger tips touch the surface of the cup."

"He's afraid of having his prints lifted," I volunteered.

Noah smiled and held the brass medallion before me as if he just caught the prized Marlin. "Sonofabitch, I got the bastard's fingerprint."

"How?"

"Before we left my house, I greased the medallion with light oil, and then I held the chain back in my palm, and draped the medallion over my finger. To the unsuspecting mind, it was like I hadn't put it back in my pocket. So when I shook hands with him, the medallion was facing just so, and I caught his thumb print right dead center."

"Did he catch on?"

Noah laughed. "Did you catch the look on his face? He knew alright, but it was already too late. What could he do?"

"Ask to see your key chain."

"Not a fucking chance. I'll bet by now he's wearing his hair shirt."

❖   ❖   ❖

Two hours had passed and Louie's house transformed into a hive of activity. The Bishop, too, was off and running from church to church, according to the Federal Agents who were tailing him. But at Louie's the gathering was turning into a procession of familiar faces and strangers, coming and going in rapid succession. Few stayed long; most were there about fifteen minutes, before taking off down the highway with an allotment of federal agents skulking on their tail.

"Looks like he went for it, big time," Noah remarked. "We're getting names and numbers that are all brand new. Pure gold!"

"Did Louie call the Bishop yet?"

"First call he made when he home. He no sooner hung up with the Bishop than the bastard took off like a striped assed ape, burning up the highway. He also bought a ticket to New York over the telephone."

"So tell me, all those C-130's, taking off and landing. Was that for real or was that all choreographed for Louie's sake?"

Noah tried to hide a very enigmatic grin.

"Doesn't really matter, does it? It achieved the results we were after."

I noticed a champagne colored Coupe de Ville Cadillac racing up the narrow road. The name Blount was inscribed on the personalized California license plates.

"That's what's his face," Noah was saying, upon spotting the car.

"Burt Blount."

"Yeah, Burt Blount, another of Louie's asshole buddies. Blount is tied into the fortress and at least one of the companies in the Roberts Trust. So that makes his appearance real interesting. The most important thing with espionage cases is to tie them in three different ways."

"What does he do? Burt's not a hitter."

"He installs fiber optic communications and security phone lines. Stuff like that; at least that's what we think. He's one of the old hands in the business. Probably he ranks above Louie in the pecking order."

I snuck up to the wall dividing Noah's property from Louie's and peeked from behind the bushes. Blount, a large man with a big, wide butt and the belly of a lapsed jock was standing in the doorway, nervously jingling the change in his pockets. He wore a cotton windbreaker that only served to accent his girth. He glanced at his watch and shuffled about impatiently. When Louie opened the door, Blount glanced around for one final look, before ducking inside.

I returned to the porch and found Noah was gone. I assumed he was inside the house eavesdropping on Louie and Burt's conversation. Although he was taping everything, Noah preferred to listen in real time every once in awhile, in case he heard something of seismic proportion. I sat back and put my feet up on the bench, contemplating at least the one lesson I had learned that day. I had learned you could feed anybody any line of bullshit, as long as you did it with true sincerity backed by the proper authority. Of course a few expensive visual props always helped to seal the deal, and it didn't hurt to take advantage of the desperation in a willing believer.

"Burt's not entirely convinced an invasion is imminent," Noah pronounced as he joined me outside. "He thinks Louie is resorting to his usual hyperbole. I'm hoping Louie will convince him that the invasion is for real."

Before either one of us could offer further insight, we heard Burt's Cadillac tearing up the driveway as if on a mission from God."

"I guess Louie came through," Noah sighed in relief.

"Our hero! Funny how they either refuse to put their trust in secure electronic communications. They are sending drivers out all over the place to hand deliver the message. What's that all about?"

"Tradition. It's what they're used to."

A few hours later Louie doused the lights in his house, started up his BMW and headed up the 405. Further north, Interstate 405 would become Interstate Five, the fastest highway to San Francisco. Louie had no idea that we were on his tail. We followed behind at a safe distance so Louie wouldn't spot Noah's white Corvette.

"Where do you think he's going?" Noah asked. It was more of a way to kill driving time than it was a serious question.

"I'll bet it's his so-called godfather. What's his face? The guy who supposedly lives up in San Francisco."

"Actually, it's further south, around Carmel and Monterey. He lives in one of those rich little towns along the coastline."

"So the plot thickens, eh? What is his name again?"

"Mark Miller. Louie calls him their family adviser. Whatever that means."

"I guess we'll find out."

"I imagine we will."

chapter

SEVENTEEN

Hours later, Louie turned off the Interstate and followed a two lane highway before making a left onto a narrow, wooded lane, servicing the large, gated estates in an exclusive coastal community known as Ocean Trails. Since we were right near the ocean, the thick layer of fog that enveloped us also hid us from any casual scrutiny. We hung well back, killing the headlights, as Louie pulled up to a gated entrance and pressed the button on the intercom. Before long, iron doors swung open, and Louie drove inside and parked his car with the other six vehicles. Noah parked about a half a block down in a place where the trees, a wall and the fog would conceal us.

"A community like this, it has to have its own security patrol," I said to Noah. "They'll be around soon enough, asking what we're doing here."

Noah fished around in the storage department for a lightweight parka and handed it to me.

"Here, take this. It'll keep you warm."

"I'm not cold."

"You will be as the night drags on. Look, I need you to hide out in the shrubbery and keep an eye on Miller's house. If anyone comes out of there, you talk to me on this."

I fished for excuses while Noah fished for a small walkie-talkie and handed it to me.

He demonstrated. "If I click twice on the transmitter, that means I want to talk to you. If you can't talk, you just click back. If you don't click back to me, I'll come in for you."

"So I sit in a clump of wet bushes all night long?"

"The coat is waterproof. It'll help."

"Help what?"

"Better leave any weapons here. The last thing we need is for a security patrol to catch you with a gun."

Noah fished around some more, and from a black nylon bag in the storage area he pulled out a Nikon 35 millimeter camera and a small pair of binoculars.

"Try to take pictures of anyone who you see coming or going. But don't take any unnecessary risks. If you are stopped, try to talk your way out of it, or escape."

"Talk my way out of it? With all this incriminating shit on me? I can see you spent a long time planning this."

Noah stared at me. I shut up. What was the sense in being sarcastic, if he wouldn't bite? After Noah indulged me with a few more nuggets of his precious wisdom, I slipped out of his car and crept down the narrow asphalt road until I reached a large clump of bushes positioned directly across from the Miller house.

I saw an opening among the trees and shrubbery and climbed inside. The leaves were wet; the ground was damp and covered with the mulch of dead leaves, branches and other organic matter I didn't wish to consider. The ground and the underbrush smelled like a cross between pond scum and sweat socks. I did my best to become one with the landscape, tucking the coat Noah had given me under the seat of my jeans. The muscles of my legs, tired from the long drive north, were starting to cramp from the cold and damp.

I spent the first hour hoping that something would happen quickly, something exciting enough to compensate for my present inertia. But soon my hope yielded to the sullen reality of a dull and wet night, in which the monotony was relieved briefly by quick glimpses of silhouettes stalking in front of the windows. Each time a figure appeared in the window I held up my binoculars in expectation that they would raise the shade for a photo opportunity. I wished they would all leave already, liberating me from the tedium and the increasingly cold weather. Occasionally, the wind picked up and blew through the bushes and the trees, sweeping water off the leaves. Onto me.

By the second hour I had determined that not only was my effort tactically important to Noah, it was also one of his periodic tests. In this case, he was proving I was soft and spoiled, and not the battle hardened spirit he pretended to revere. Noah thought this was a sure way of getting under my skin, inducing me to prove myself by performing improbable tasks for illogical reasons. He believed he was subtle enough that I didn't see through his nonsense, but I did. I took the bait anyway, or at least about fifty percent of the time. And in this case, I assured myself I would prove that these climatic assaults against body and soul were only minor distractions. My spirit would endure. To dispel the creature discomforts I confronted, I summoned whatever Zen-like tidbits I had plucked from the metaphysical swap meet, along with inspirational dialogue from the syndicated reruns of Kung Fu that I could still remember.

During the third hour it occurred to me that what I was doing was potentially dangerous. Had I been spotted by any one of these assholes, Louie would have identified me, and I would probably be shot. Or worse. I found it vaguely amusing that in all my concern for the monotony, drudgery and general discomfort, the threat of violence against me hadn't crossed my mind. My amusement would soon transform into borderline terror.

The meeting was finally breaking up. Eight men filed out of the house, shaking hands all around. Setting down my binoculars, I picked up the camera and starting taking pictures, focusing on Miller, who stood in the driveway bidding everyone goodbye. I could tell by his posture that he considered himself the big cheese. Louie was the last to leave—he and a bespectacled figure in a dark raincoat, slouched brim hat and a long scarf wrapped strategically around his face.

I got on the walkie-talkie and whispered. "Noah, are you there?"

"I'm here."

I was relieved to hear his voice.

"They're breaking up. There's about eight of them. Louie is with this one guy, I can't tell who he is. He has his collar hiked up and a scarf wrapped around his face."

"Can you get out of there?"

"Not likely."

"Then wait. Get license plates."

"I'm trying," I said, taking pictures of the cars pulling out of the driveway.

Louie was the last to pull out, and Miller retreated back inside his house. A moment later the house went dark. It was like someone had pulled a master switch, killing all the lights at once. I felt eyes on me.

"You still there?"

"Give me a minute. Miller could be watching me."

"I'm coming in."

"No, don't. It'll blow everything. Let me think."

Suddenly, it wasn't such a bright idea not to be armed, although I was quite certain Miller was far better trained with weapons than I was. I switched off the walkie-talkie and started crawling through the clump of bushes, moving deliberately so as not to rustle the leaves. I took my time, picking my way across the saturated landscape, barely able to see a foot or so in front of my eyes. I felt branches scratch my hands and face, but I crawled on until I was able to slide out from a space in the brush at the rear of the building. There a seven-foot wall ran the perimeter of a neighboring house and confronted me with ornate pointed iron spikes running along its top. I removed Noah's coat and threw it over the spikes for cushioning, and then leapt up and swung myself over the wall. I lost my balance midway, and it was all I could do to keep my feet when I landed. I was not the cat burglar that I had hoped to be. A clumsy move, for sure. But it was also the right one.

No sooner had I landed than I heard dogs. There were two of them on leashes, being trailed by a high-powered light beam and Miller with a gun. Hell Hounds on My Trail, suddenly popped inside my head. I wasted no time running toward the rear of the yard, pulling my walkie-talkie as I neared the back wall.

"Can you read me?"

"Yes. Where are you?"

"I will be coming out one road west of our house. That is one road closer to the Pacific. You'd better be there in a hurry. Copy? Or whatever the fuck you say into this thing."

As I reached the back wall, I turned and saw a light beam waving around in the darkness. I heard the dogs barking; only now the dogs were closer. If Miller released the dogs from their leashes, they would be on me in seconds. I raced across to the opposite fence and again slipped the coat on top of the spikes, grabbed the wrought iron and pulled myself over. When I landed on the other side, I heard a car engine approaching. Noah stopped long enough for me to get in, and then he took off down the tree-lined road. Despite the fog and darkness, he negotiated the wet asphalt, trees and narrow turns with an expert's skill.

"Miller was onto me," I said. "I don't know if it was a night vision scope or if heard me talking into the walkie-talkie. Otherwise I never made a sound, never even stirred. He just sensed I was there."

"Did you get pictures?"

"Yeah, I did. I could really use a cup of coffee."

"Sorry, but we've got to get on Louie's tail. My gut tells me he's carrying precious cargo."

"You saw him?"

"He drove right by me. I was parked in the driveway of a vacant house."

"How do you know which way he's going?"

"He's going north. I just know it."

chapter

EIGHTEEN

Noah was right. We picked up Louie's BMW near Castroville, just as he turned off the Coastal Highway and headed north on Interstate 101. A couple of hours later we were tailing him into San Francisco. It was the middle of the night when we crossed over the Oakland-East Bay Bridge, and scant traffic occupied the city streets. We still kept a discrete distance behind Louie's BMW as he entered the heart of the Richmond district of San Francisco.

"Figures," said Noah. "The Chinese neighborhood."

"No. We're not close to Chinatown."

"Naw, that's for the tourists and the hard cases. It's cramped and archaic, and there's too much crime. "This is where the middle class actually lives."

The Richmond section, with its expansive Edwardian houses and modern apartments, offered greater space and less distraction and a commercial section more suitable for Chinese business transactions. In the probable case of Louie's passenger, the Richmond was a great place to blend in unnoticed.

Louie pulled up to a once stately Edwardian house that had years ago suffered the commercial ignominy of being converted to apartments. We drove past and parked the car further down the street, where we were partially concealed by shrouds of thick, heavy fog that was rolling in from the Pacific Ocean. We watched Louie and his passenger in the rear and side view mirrors. A few minutes passed, and nobody got out of Louie's car.

"What do you think is going on in there?"

"Louie is doing his Louie number. Probably selling him one last time on how valuable a resource Louie is."

A moment later the mysterious passenger climbed out of the car, a suitcase in hand. He approached the Edwardian building and rang one of several apartment doorbells. The door opened and he went inside.

"Could you tell which apartment he went into?"

"Not from this angle. I haven't seen any new lights go on in the building either. Whoever it is inside, is obviously expecting him."

"Take a look at the mailboxes, and write down the names."

I started out of the car, but quickly closed the door and ducked down in the seat.

"Louie's heading this way."

Noah tilted over in his seat and covered his head just as the headlights on Louie's BMW pulled alongside, and Louie slowed down just enough for a better look.

"If he gets out of the car, we are fucked."

"If he gets out of the car, he's dead," Noah informed me. It was an even more obvious fact than the one I had pointed out.

But Louie, as luck would have it, drove on.

"Is he blessed, or what?"

"Now where the hell is he going?"

Noah heard me, but he was too deep in his thoughts to answer the question.

"I guess we'd better follow him."

Louie drove directly back to the Haight Ashbury section and parked near renovated Victorian house that stood off Haight Street about midway up the hill. The Victorian house had been treated recently to a special paint job, in the multi-colored and gold leaf tradition of its gingerbread architecture. The older windows had been refinished or replaced with new ones that were now protected against burglary with metal bars over the glass. A heavy steel mesh door dissuaded forcible intrusion. I noticed a wooden relief of a now familiar symbol was positioned over the entrance. I also noticed antenna sprouting from the roof. Quite to my surprise, we were staring at consecrated ground.

"You figured this is out yet?"

"I know this is a branch of the Old Holy Church. Looks like Louie is planning to stay the night."

"I'd love to get a look at the people inside."

We watched in silence as Louie got out of his car, dragging a gym bag out of his trunk.

"How many guns do you think are in that bag?"

No sooner had Louie reached the porch than a light came on and a man appeared in the open doorway. We couldn't hear what they said to each other, but it was clear the man was expecting Louie. He stepped aside, and Louie ducked inside the house.

"Shit, I wish you could find a hidden spot to watch this place. While I went back and kept my eye on Louie's passenger."

"Are you kidding? At the very least, I'd get mugged around here."

Noah thought it over by touching his tongue to the roof of his mouth, making a clucking sound that was on the brink of annoying.

"I guess we should get a motel somewhere. I need to make a few phone calls on a secure land line, and maybe we can squeeze in a couple hours sleep."

We found one of the many nondescript motels on Lombard Street, and while Noah talked on the phone, I grabbed a couple of hours sleep. I was finally able to slip off my damp clothes and crawl into fabric that was warm and dry. The mattress was old and lumpy, and the pillow stank faintly of tobacco smoke and genital sweat from a lot of someone else's drunken nights of reverie. I didn't care. I slept in light and restless cycles. Vaguely I heard Noah's voice as he made one call and then another. I could tell by the tone of his voice that we were onto big stuff. With me he often tended to minimize our discoveries, but with his colleagues it was sometimes a different matter. With them he would stress their importance.

It was just before dawn when Noah peeled back the draperies and told me it was time to wake up.

"It's still dark out," I complained.

"We have work to do."

I got up and rubbed my eyes. My tongue was rough and dry, and it felt like I had been using it to dig my way through freshly dredged river silt. I felt dirty and greasy, and suffered from severe bed head with my hair curled and twisted in every direction.

"What's the matter?"

"I feel like shit."

"Perfect. I want you to stay just like you are."

"C'mon, Noah, I have to shower."

"No, you can't shower."

"Why's that?"

"Because you look like a derelict, and that's just the look you'll need to get inside the Church."

I shook my head. "Louie is in the Church. He'll spot me."

"He's already gone. Back to LA."

"You're sure?"

"Feds are on his tail."

"Well, I'm always happy to see my tax dollars in action."

"Come on," said Noah. "I'll buy you breakfast, and then we'll get down to work."

In still damp jeans and too light a jacket, I went with Noah to eat in a nearby greasy spoon where they serve that nationally famous breakfast special: eggs, potatoes, toast and bacon for something like two ninety-five. We sat in a booth in the rear by the window, where under harsh fluorescent lights we wolfed down greasy food and bad coffee and watched the sun rise upon the city.

"We're getting a lot from this session with Louie," Noah whispered, leaning over the table. Back east, we've discovered two Chinese Nationals, cultural attaches, that are directly involved. They have been identified as operatives at Level T, the Dragon Squad, which is equivalent to the First Directorate, Line R of the KGB."

"Which is...?"

"Technical intelligence mainly. And occasional wet work. One is probably a colonel in rank, and the other is his junior officer. They had a meeting with what's his face, Clifton, the supposed student living at Louie's house. After their meeting, they returned to the office and spoke for over two hours on a secure phone line. Then they drove up through Yonkers, spreading the word about the Nicaragua invasion. They changed cars three times to blow off any surveillance. But our guys stayed on them and followed them to a mix of Chinese restaurants, antique shops and a newsstand, six places in all. At least five of their contacts were new to our agents."

I nodded. "There's more. You were on the phone an awfully long time."

"We spotted three other Chinese nationals going out from their New York Consulate. They went north as far as Massachusetts, and as far south as Camden, New Jersey. We also found another Church in Albany, New York."

"Add in our finds up here. So far, we have visited church, the consulate and that apartment over in the Richmond section."

Noah smiled, exhaling a steady stream of cigarette smoke. "Meanwhile, I'm dying to know the identity of our mystery man and what he is all about."

Stubbing out his cigarette butt in one of those cheap tin ashtrays, Noah reached into his pocket and pulled out a roll of cash, an act that wasn't lost on the few motley early birds who made this place their regular morning stop.

"Better be cool with that money," I admonished.

Noah acknowledged me with a perfunctory nod as he slid across the booth and struggled to his feet. He glanced around, adjusting his collar, his eyes shooting a warning that if you started with him, you faced death. Not a word was spoken, but I saw eyes look away. Clearly they had gotten the message.

The thick morning fog had barely begun to recede as the first of the homeless, the restless and the shiftless began to congregate on Haight Street. Despite the nascent attempts at neighborhood gentrification, the lost children huddled on the sidewalk and pressed their backs against the graffiti-ridden walls, sipping coffee from Styrofoam cups, eating doughnuts and smoking cigarettes. The alcoholics among the crowd swigged on that first-of-the-morning bottle of beer they had bought with greasy change from the nearby convenience store. There they were, the young gutter trash mixing with the aging remnants of the left over hippies, relics of neo-American tribal living that had been hyped by the media pundits a couple of decades earlier. I had spent a couple of months up there, during the Summer of Love. Talk about some ancient history.

I studied the assorted derelicts carefully, paying special attention to their movement and their posture, knowing later that day I would be emulating their habits on the steps of the Church for the benefit of my country. It was beyond irony that acting the part of a disposable miscreant was my contribution to the security of this great nation. I slouched my shoulders and hung my arms, trying to replicate that semi-squinting, passive aggressive expression most wore on their face.

"What the fuck are you doing?" Noah asked, snapping me out of my thoughts.

"Rehearsing my part as a bum. You want me to be convincing, don't you?"

"Alright. Meanwhile we have some time to kill. I have a hunch. Let's try something else."

chapter

NINETEEN

The San Francisco Chinese Consulate was situated in an old mission style office building at the corner of Laguna and Geary. The Consulate looked ordinary enough, had not dozens of antennas and a few satellite dishes prickled out from its rooftop, picking up every burp, fart and techie talk from, say, the Silicon Valley. Of course, while particular attention was paid to America's technological vanguard, other Northern California corporate telephone conversations were far from neglected. The rooftop installation, Noah told me, also included the apparatus necessary to send and receive ultra-secure communiqués from both the homeland and the Chinese satellites flying overhead. In fact, inside that building there was a small slice of sovereign

China, and the people responsible took that and their subsequent information gathering very seriously.

After all, this was politically active San Francisco, and the Chinese Consulate had endured its fair share of demonstrations in which hundreds and thousands protested China's religious and cultural oppression as well as my personal favorite blight on humanity, slave labor. Such demonstrations had long ago intensified internal security, and anyone who lingered out front or walked by at frequent intervals was immediately placed under surveillance by the guards and the miniature cameras hidden inside the building.

"It's the Chinese headquarters for spying on the technological centers in Northern California and the Pacific Northwest."

"Yeah, but then what are we doing sitting outside?"

"Since I convinced Louie we were invading Nicaragua, this place has been a beehive of activity. You noticed all those antennas up on the roof?"

By now I was getting good at counting phone lines and antennas.

"Yes. Of course."

"We wait here long enough, and we'll light onto something. I have an affinity for drawing intrigue right into my lap. It happens to me all over the world. Others could be sitting around for ages and nothing would happen. But me, I'd no sooner go somewhere and all of a sudden, I'd be surrounded by intrigue of one sort or another."

"Maybe you just imagine it."

Noah shot me a look.

"Just kidding."

I was. I had been around Noah long enough to know better, and I bore witness to how Louie Dubin had the piss poor sense to move in next door.

"What I'd pay to eavesdrop on those signals," Noah sighed wistfully. Especially when they communicate with their satellites."

"I thought our satellites could eavesdrop on theirs."

"Can't break the codes. Not yet, anyway…Goddammit! I'd love to hear what they are saying about Nicaragua."

"Why are the Chinese so concerned over Nicaragua?"

"Like I told you, Nicaragua is the only place we can build a new canal. Meanwhile the Chinese are doing everything they can to position themselves strategically. They're even making a lot of moves in Panama."

"The Panama Canal? That's our domain."

"Remember, we're turning it back to the Panamanians. That leaves the door open, especially if the PRC exerts enough economic clout over Panama."

Noah shook his head, and several moments lapsed in awkward silence.

"What? What is it?"

He gestured toward the Consulate. "Chinese agents have been coming and going, traipsing all over the Silicon Valley with near impunity. Either they are protected by diplomatic appointment, or by good old American lethargy. We just sit like idiots on our ass. All this time they've been ripping us off, improving their technology and their weapons systems on our dime. And a lot of it right from that building."

Not fifteen seconds later, our Mystery Man from the night before strode purposely out of the Consulate and walked north on Laguna. He was coming right toward us, carrying a small suitcase, the one from the night before.

"What's this now?" Noah pondered.

Our Mystery Man was dressed in the same long overcoat, a wide brimmed hat, and sunglasses. To conceal himself better, he had hiked up his coat collar and wrapped a scarf around the lower section of his face. If he recognized us from the night before, he gave no sign of it as he walked quickly past us.

"Better get out and see where he goes," Noah ordered. "I'll go around the block and meet you further up the street."

"If he turns the corner?"

"I'll find you," Noah assured me as he waved me out of the car.

I got out of the car and followed our Mystery Man. Determined not to lose him, I quickened my pace to close the distance. But no sooner had I drawn close, than a beige Toyota swung round the corner and pulled up to the curb next to our Mystery Man. Without hesitation he scrambled inside, and the Toyota pulled out into traffic. I lowered my head as the car drove past, weighing the odds that they hadn't spotted me.

Noah pulled his Corvette up alongside me, and I jumped in.

"See, what did I tell you about my affinity?"

"Did you see how he was dressed? With a wide brimmed hat, yet. Truth is, the scarf and the sunglasses make him that much more obvious."

"He would rather look obvious than risk being identified. That probably means he is here illegally. In fact, I'd bet a dollar to a soggy doughnut that he snuck into the country. I'll bet another buck he's no small operator."

Traffic was heavy, but Noah managed to stay several cars behind him. The Toyota took a left toward the ocean, and we followed.

"I'd love to get that suitcase," Noah pronounced, all revved up from the thrill of the chase. "If we get the chance, we'll take him."

"And if he runs? I'm not what you call the fastest man on earth, and you can hardly walk."

"Don't worry about me, Sonny Boy. I can move, if I have to."

There was no sense in arguing, and for all I knew Noah could actually summon preternatural strength that would allow him to give chase after the younger man. I shut up and watched the Toyota weave in and out of the traffic, moving just fast enough to make us wonder whether or not he had picked up our tail. I guessed that he had, but decided it was best to keep that opinion to myself. We drove for a couple of miles, back toward the Richmond Section.

"Maybe we'll catch a break, and we'll be able to follow him back to that house."

But that was not to be the case. Once inside the Richmond district, the Toyota pulled into a gated underground parking garage that serviced a multiple story apartment complex.

"He's smart," Noah acknowledged as we drove right on past the apartment complex's gated entrance. "He's also jumpy and probably suspicious enough to have picked up our tail. Or he makes it his habit not to sleep in the same place twice. Who the fuck is this guy, anyway?"

"So now what?"

"In a place this size he'll be awfully hard to find."

"Plan B."

"It involves me, doesn't it?"

Noah smiled like a happy lawn gnome. "Hell yeah, you're the star attraction."

A few blocks down on Clement Street, Noah parked near a pay phone and got out to make a few calls. Clement Street had its share off brand and surplus stores that sold assorted goods from China.

"Why not use a cell phone?" I wondered aloud. The answer was pretty much what I expected.

"Too easy to tap into your call."

He was surely the expert on radio transmission and its encompassing higher technologies, so I didn't see the point in asking further questions.

"While you make your calls, I'm going to stop in one of these stores and pick up some warm and dry clothing."

"Wait," he said, reaching into his pocket. He pulled out a hundred dollar bill and handed it to me. "Get me a sweater or sweatshirt and a couple clean pairs of socks."

I stood there, not knowing if I should buy my clothes as well as his with the hundred. Or just his. Noah could be lavish at times, but mostly, with the exception of his electronics and computers, he drifted toward the cheap side. I decided, screw it. After all this, the least that he owed me was a clean pair of jeans.

I stopped in the first of several Asian surplus shops where they sold everything from cooking spoons to rainwear, which they bought as overruns and closeouts for a few cents on the dollar. It was the Chinese manufacturer's way of making an extra buck—overproducing a brand name product and then selling the surplus to his state side relatives or, for that matter, any schmuck with a flea market space. While scoping the aisles, I glanced out the window and noticed a BMW moving slowly down the street. A Chinese man and woman were teamed in the car, and although they pretended not to take much notice of me, I could sense they were tailing us. My first guess was our Mystery Man had called in reinforcements.

In that first rush of paranoia I speculated that I had somehow been set up and that the shopkeeper was in on it, and in lieu of the old San Francisco tradition of being shanghaied and put on a sailing ship bound for who knows where, I would merely be rendered into fish food and dropped in the evening tide. But I stopped worrying about the shopkeeper when I saw his stern face was more concerned with making sure Noah's hundred wasn't counterfeit than he was with any elaborate kidnap plans.

"You have something smaller?" he demanded.

"Sorry."

He scowled once more at my ratty appearance. After performing every test he could think of, he accepted the bill for a pair of counterfeit Calvin Klein jeans, a couple of navy sweatshirts, some socks and, as a special treat, a couple pairs of knock-off underwear. On shear impulse I bought baseball type caps and two cheap pairs of gloves. The bill was less than fifty bucks.

I made my way out the door, half expecting to find the Chinese guy lurking outside. Instead he was parked down the street with the woman at the wheel. When she saw me, she lifted a camera and tried to take my picture. I turned and pretended to scratch my cheek, covering my face with one of the shopping bags. I tried to make the move look incidental, but I doubt seriously that she bought it. Out of the corner of my eye, I caught what I could of their license plate number and committed it to memory. Turning up the street, I headed back toward where Noah had parked. He was already waiting in the Corvette.

"We've got company," I said, slipping the bags in the trunk. "A Chinese couple in a BMW."

"This should be fun," Noah pronounced phlegmatically as I climbed inside the car. "Better buckle your seatbelt."

He pulled out of his parking space and drove slowly down Clement Street with the couple in the BMW falling in several cars behind.

"You want their license number?"

"Already have it. Did they take your picture?"

"They tried. I turned away."

"Hell, don't you want to be famous back in China?"

"That's me. Prince of the Forbidden City."

Noah signaled a left toward the park and waited in the turn lane until after the yellow light turned red, before making his turn. As we expected, the BMW followed.

"You ready to lose him?" Noah asked me.

"Can we do it like Steve McQueen did in Bullit? It would be one major rush to go flying up over these hills."

"Bottoms out your suspension and ruins your car," Noah answered as he approached the base of the hill.

"You're always so practical. Steve McQueen wouldn't worry about his suspension. He'd just want to look cool."

That was all I needed to say. Suddenly Noah mashed the pedal to the floor, and the Corvette squealed, burning serious rubber as it started to climb. As he neared the top of the hill, Noah hung a quick right down a side street and went bouncing down the hill, sometimes blindly leaping wildly across the intersections and picking up speed. We flashed by moving cars and commercial trucks, dodged the intersecting traffic. Perhaps I should have been frightened, but I wasn't. I figured Noah had endured enough serious injury throughout his life that at this juncture a little joyride like this one would never result in the final adventure. Besides, at his age and at this stage, let the man enjoy himself a little.

I turned and looked out the rear window to see how the older and less powerful BMW was making out with the car chase. As we neared the bottom of the hill, Noah swung a hard left down another side street, almost reducing the San Francisco population by a few preoccupied pedestrians. He floored it in the direction of Golden Gate Park.

"Car really hauls ass."

"It's not just the car," he reminded. "It's also the driver."

Again I looked behind us. The Chinese driver was losing ground.

"Is he still behind us?"

It was a rhetorical question. Noah could see him easily in his rearview mirror.

"After a fashion."

"Good. I wouldn't want to lose him, until he really feels humiliated. You think the broad is giving him any shit?"

"She's not giving him any head. Not on this bumpy ride."

Noah entered Golden Gate Park at eighty miles an hour, weaving in and out of traffic as he turned into the twisting side roads that wound throughout the park. He was having fun now; I could see it on his face. By the time we emerged on the south side of Golden Gate Park, the BMW was little more than a memory.

chapter

TWENTY

Night fell and the fog rolled in, filling the valleys and covering the bridges and buildings like a persistent legend that was true and yet, by morning, untraceable. The streets were wet and the city was cold, the kind of chill that pierced the thickest of jackets and the toughest of souls. I could feel the dampness in my jeans again, and the wet air reminded me that I stank of B.O. and my clothes felt glued to my skin. I could easily die of crotch rot.

Noah dropped me off a couple of blocks from the Church, and I walked the rest of the way, making sure I wouldn't be the first to arrive. I hoped to be just one among the crowd, barely noticed as I took my seat. Once there, I expected to find your usual garden variety of bums and winos, derelicts and homeless. And while I did see a few of the dispossessed, I realized most in attendance were mannered and clean like respectable citizens. They were dressed in the polo shirts, plaids and khakis of mid-level techies, or in bargain suits from off brand stores. I disguised my surprise in a custom crafted aura of self possession and existential misery, keeping my head down and my eyes on the floor as I passed through the entrance and the scrutiny of the priest taking the head count out on the porch.

"Good to see you here," the good father greeted me.

I nodded obliquely and acted like it was questionable if I really had heard him or not. I felt his eyes all over me, as I deliberately glazed over my own so I looked disconnected to the world around me. We moved into what used to be the living and dining rooms, and possibly a study, where the inner walls had been knocked down in favor of open space. There was a pulpit situated at one side of the room, set before rows of folding chairs. Floral patterned wallpaper covered one wall, and the others were painted the shade of cheap mint green bad decorators tell you is easy on the eyes. On either side of the space there were bookshelves and a pair of second hand tables. One served as a coffee and doughnut stand, and the other as a repository for the numerous rambling and seemingly illogical religious tracts the Bishop had given me.

The better-washed and better-attired practitioners of this esoteric faith were busy gathering the religious tracts. A scant few, if any, bothered to even briefly read the headings on the tracts or thumb through the content. They just stuffed them neatly in their pockets or the portfolios and briefcases they had brought along for the task. I noticed a few of the faithful were of Chinese heritage.

On the other hand, the few derelicts ignored the tracts and competed instead for the jelly doughnuts and coffee.

I moved closer to the table and, to the surprise of most that were gathered there, picked up multiple copies of all seven tracts and slipped them into my mud crusted jacket. One of the topics that aroused my interest—When the Clergy Sanctions Violence—was a popular issue. I searched the table for When the Clergy Sanctions Self-Abuse. But I suppose that one was out of print.

"They keep me warm," I mumbled, demonstrating how I packed them under my clothes to the inquisitive soul in the ugly plaid jacket and spectacles standing just to my left. He nodded, neither understanding the concept, nor wanting to delve into it further.

Organ music kicked in from a cheap Casio keyboard, and everybody took his or her seat. The more respectable turned right to the appropriate page in the photocopied prayer book, while the derelicts fumbled with doughnuts and coffee, spilling powdered sugar onto the pages. Having watched this happen more than a few times, I fingered my prayer book. Many of the pages were sticky like the kiddy magazines in a pediatrician's office.

We sang a few prayers in English, and the crisp and toneless techies harmonized strangely with a lagging wino chorus, so that the end result was a kind of weird and syncopated droning. I wondered what God must have thought about this odd and off key assemblage beseeching him for the usual favors. We listened to a ten-minute talk about the soul, salvation and an unremarkable synopsis of the trials and tribulations of the world. There was, however, a colorful discussion after that. I found it particularly compelling since the crack heads and winos were trying desperately to express themselves in slurred language and tangential thought patterns. For dramatic counterpoint a trio of drugged out hookers launched into a series of erratic and sometimes graphic confessions about sin and life on the street.

As the service ended, I took my cue from the Casio organ music and stood up and started to wander around. I was hoping to gain entrance to the basement, but a cleric stood in my path as a clear obstruction to the descending staircase. Yet another cleric protected the upstairs so that the only access was to the exit or the good father who led the service. I drew bad coffee from the large urn and leaned against the wall, observing carefully how the better heeled among the congregation gathered their things, bid goodbye and hurried out the door.

I was slow to notice the Mystery Man Louie had been chauffeuring around as he ascended from the basement and paused at the top of the stairs. When I turned in his direction, I found him staring at me. He wore neither his hat nor his sunglasses, and I was able to snatch a quick and careful peek at his intelligent and sensitive face. He was a handsome Chinese man, with the bearing of a patrician born to the upper echelons of the communist hive. He carried his hat in his hand, and his overcoat and scarf dangled from the crook of his arm.

Rather than avert my eyes, I put on my best glazed over expression and stared right back and through him, as if he wasn't even there. I remained like that for considerable time, pretending to be deep in drug related reverie, unaware of anything but that far distant image that had captured my attention. Still, I felt him looking me over until some guy in a dark green blazer and toothy grin interrupted him. Whether the Mystery Man had recognized me, or whether I had merely aroused his curiosity, it was hard to tell.

A few moments later I was back on the street. I shuffled like the lost soul I was pretending to be in the direction where I knew Noah would be waiting. When I spotted his car, with only the slightest nod I walked on by. If Noah was nothing, he was quick on the uptake, and that quickly he got the message that someone could be following me. He hung back; making sure no one was on my tail, before picking me up a block from where I had turned onto Haight Street.

"Any luck?" he asked as soon as I climbed into his Corvette.

I removed the religious tracts from my jacket and showed them to him.

"All of the more respectable assholes were taking these. They never bothered to thumb through them or read them. They just picked them up and put them in their briefcases. I thought that was pretty strange.

"And by the way, when the service ended, I noticed our Mystery Man coming up the basement staircase. I was able to catch a glimpse of his face."

"You would recognize him again?"

I nodded. "Count on it."

"Tell me again about these tracts. Where were they?"

"On a table. Coffee and doughnuts were on a table on one side, and the tracts on the other. The derelicts went for the coffee and doughnuts, the faithful went for these."

I watched his eyes light up and the turbine engines crank inside his brain. He smiled, which for Noah was practically beaming.

"This is it," he proclaimed, tapping the tracts.

"Yeah? What?"

"These are the scratch sheets. This is how they communicate."

"The codes. These books are coded. All of them?"

"Probably. They probably work the tracts in a cycle of some kind."

"So these are their version of secret decoder rings?"

Noah nodded. "Precisely. I think we got them, finally."

"You don't know the codes though."

"I will. A dollar to a soggy doughnut says I'll have the codes before the month is out."

"Great. Can I change now?"

"Not until tomorrow. There is something else I need you to do."

"The Mystery Man."

"Unless I miss my guess, he'll be coming out of the consulate the same time he did today."

"What makes you think that?"

"You see by his actions, all very deliberate. The way he adjusts his hat, fixes his glasses. He is not a very spontaneous man. There is even a regular precision to the way he tries to throw us off his track. We've got to find out who he is and what he's doing here."

"And we can't do that if I'm washed and dressed in clean clothes."

"The Navy SEALs go for days crawling in mud, setting fuses in fifty degree water. They lay in the ocean for hours on end, and you know how cold that is."

"That's nothing. I can lie around in bed for days."

He shrugged. "Just look at it as part of the job."

I nodded. It was an argument I would never win.

chapter

TWENTY-ONE

Late the following afternoon we found ourselves perched once again parked up the block from the Chinese Consulate. If Noah were correct, then our Mystery Man would soon be emerging from the Chinese Consulate to be whisked away by the same Toyota that picked him up the day before. We watched and we waited, and I fingered the untraceable Colt .38 snub nose revolver Noah had lent me for this particular occasion.

"Are you sure you are up to this?" he asked again. I could tell by his tone of voice that this was not one more of his famous challenges, but this time he was worried about my well being.

"Am I sure? Not really. It's not like I have ever done this before. I can't say it fills me with that warm all over glow."

"Just remember. You're doing it for your country."

"Thanks. That helps a lot. Before, I was just nervous. Now I am nervous and patriotic. You sure there isn't someone else who can do this?"

He frowned at my sarcasm. "You're doing what's necessary. It's part of the bigger picture. And we are short a man."

"I understand. I know. We've been through the pep rally a dozen times already. Still doesn't mean I feel good about it."

"I've done hundreds of things that have turned my stomach. This is nothing by comparison."

"It shows on you," I wanted to say, but respect and civility prevented me from doing so. Instead I looked Noah up and down, noted the tell tale signs that were etched on his soul. Physically, those signs were manifested in scars and bullet holes, shriveled legs and that perpetually exhausted look of carrying the weight of the world on his shoulders. But I knew the wounds ran much deeper than mere surface disfigurements. The sad fact of it all— he had born this weight so long he sincerely believed it was a natural state of being.

"You really think he's that much the heavy?" I was asking as much to change the subject as to gain any assurance.

Noah paused to light up a cigarette. "We're dealing with top shelf here," he replied, exhaling a column of smoke. "I can feel it."

Noah looked away, considering how to express his point.

"He's trying so hard not to be noticed, he's become obvious. And that is his big mistake."

I stared through the windshield in search of the Toyota. Sure enough, it was coming up the street, moving slowly so to time perfectly its pickup. A woman in sunglasses was driving, her two hands on the wheel. She was staring straight ahead, suspecting nothing. I sensed she was not really new at this game, but she wasn't exactly a veteran either. I couldn't tell if she had locked the car doors. I was betting she hadn't. Betting heavily, since my mission largely depended on it.

"You'd better get going," Noah informed me, as if he was sending me for a pizza that threatened to grow stale under the infrared warming lights.

I got out of his car, shelving my concerns about the ambiguousness of morality, the virtues of right and wrong. I worked hard, overcoming fears and sucking up my courage as I advanced on the Toyota. While crossing the street I noticed our Mystery Man was emerging from the Chinese Consulate, right on cue. He was walking swiftly toward the rendezvous point. I quickened my pace, grateful she was stalling in heavy traffic.

I met the Toyota as it made its turn at the corner. Yanking open the passenger door, I drew my pistol from my pocket and swung inside the car. The Chinese driver reached frantically for her handbag, but I snatched it from her grasp. I stuck the pistol in her face and tried to act tough. I didn't think I was doing that good of a job. Her eyes darted from my face to the gun as she deliberated on her options. For a horrifying moment I thought she was going to laugh.

"Drive!" I demanded, gesturing for her to continue down Post. Or I'll put a bullet right in your fucking head!"

She glowered at me, looking me up and down, wondering if I would really make good on my threat. Since I was smelly and soiled, all nasty looking with my hair stiff and greasy, I made for a much more credible miscreant. Noah had been wise in forbidding me to shower. My stink alone could render her helpless.

"Get out of this car!" she commanded in near perfect English.

"Drive," I ordered, trying to sell her that I wasn't fooling around.

"Fuck you!" she shrieked. She was so loud, my ears were ringing.

It was her mistake. She had pissed me off. In desperation, I cracked the gun against her forehead and spoke through gritted teeth.

"I won't tell you again. Move this motherfucking car!"

She was glancing over my shoulder, glimpsing the approaching Mystery Man. He was still too far away to do any good. For the first time she looked worried. She cursed me in what I assumed was Chinese. The spot I had cracked her was turning red and beginning to swell. She turned to me, staring daggers.

I jammed the gun against her temple and cocked the hammer. "I said move it!"

A gasping sigh of deep remorse escaped from her mouth as she took one final look in the direction of the Mystery Man before slipping the car into drive. As we pulled out and crossed the street, I caught a glimpse of the Mystery Man, frozen and dumbfounded, realizing he had just been stranded.

"Where are you taking me?" the woman demanded.

"Just keep driving."

"You won't hurt me," she said more to assure herself than to admonish me. "Not for this old car. It's a piece of shit."

"I don't want your car," I whispered.

That got her eyes to popping. She realized this was far more serious than a mere carjacking. She gritted her teeth and cursed again in Chinese as she followed traffic for another dozen blocks. Further south of the Consulate I ordered her to pull into a side street and finally into a driveway that was obscure in the lengthening shadows of the afternoon. We were out of the line of sight of any curious bystanders.

"Give me the keys!"

She pulled them from the ignition and handed them over. Her hands were shaking now.

"Please don't kill me," she pleaded, the first hint of fear and desperation creeping into her voice.

"Just keep your hands on your head," I told her as I snatched up her purse, backed out of the car and came around to the driver's side.

She was looking back and forth from the pistol to my face, trying to predict her future. I ordered her out of the car, and she watched nervously as I popped open the trunk.

"Get in there," I demanded.

"Why?"

I sensed from the horror on her face she may have suffered from claustrophobia.

"Either get in the fucking trunk, or I shoot you."

Suddenly the trunk appeared much more attractive to her. She climbed in, moving quickly and gracefully, and as she raised her skirt so not to muss it, I noticed her legs were shapely and strong. I wondered if she was a former gymnast or a martial arts specialist who, had I not had the gun, would have gladly kicked my ass.

"You'll be sorry for this," she promised as she climbed inside.

I closed the trunk lid. Stuffing the pistol in my jacket, I backed off down the street where a helmeted man on a motorcycle was waiting to meet me. Between the helmet and the dark, sunshade visor, I never did see his face. He was my backup and followed me, just in case. I sensed if I had screwed up my first carjacking, he was there to kill the Chinese woman and preserve whatever chance they had at the Mystery Man.

As I approached, the man on the bike handed me a helmet. I climbed on the back, and we drove off. Shortly after, we were back on Lombard Street, and the driver pulled into the parking lot of one of the dozens of nondescript motels positioned on either side of the street.

The man on the bike handed me a key to one of the rooms.

"There's a bag inside your room, along with your change of clothes. Take off everything you are wearing, put it in the bag and give it to me. Including the gun."

Once inside the room, I stripped quickly, and with a towel wrapped around my waist I handed him the woman's purse and the bag of funky clothing. I wiped the gun and everything else clean of prints, before I handed it over. He snatched it from me and took off for parts unknown. I settled in for a long, hot shower, letting the steam build in the bathroom; the heat was easing my tension. I shaved and changed into the fresh clothing, the stuff I had bought earlier that day. I flicked on the TV and tried not to think about my carjacking venture, but visions of the incident kept invading my brain.

I was grateful the woman hadn't really tested me and that at the end of the day the woman and I were both still alive. I flicked on the evening news and waited for Noah. An hour passed, and then two. I resigned myself to a long wait, hoping on his end of it things had gone according to plan.

Just after eight I heard Noah's Corvette rumble up to the entrance. I opened the door for him, watching as he struggled out of his car and shuffled inside the motel room. He was glancing at me with that now familiar look, as if he was trying to determine what planet I was from.

"Did it go alright?"

"Not bad for a beginner. What about you?"

He sat down and pulled a cigarette from his pack, fished for his disposable lighter. He lit up, luxuriating in that first bit of toxic waste.

"Our Mystery Man did not survive a terrible mugging. That big briefcase he was carrying? He wouldn't give it up. Had he dropped it, he probably would have gotten away.

"The boys chased him down and cornered him in an alley. He put up one helluva fight, until one of our men caught him with a chop to his carotid artery."

"So he's dead?"

"Depends on how you look at it."

"What's that supposed to mean?"

"To deceive the Chinese, we put someone who looks like him on a plane bound for Taiwan. As far as anyone is concerned, he defected to the West. It would be the shits if they realized he's dead."

"Are you sure they'll buy it? His driver, the woman I hijacked, will be telling her version of the story."

Noah sat on the edge of the bed. "Well, yeah, but she died tragically from carbon monoxide poisoning. Not that it matters what she died from. They'll never find either body."

I sat surprised and silent, absorbing the new twist on things. My role as a carjacker had wrought greater consequence than I had expected. With that new understanding, I had visions of the Chinese woman lying in the truck, battling her claustrophobia, relieved that she had survived a carjacking. And then with no warning, with the exception perhaps of a slamming car door, her Toyota was driven to some isolated spot and the trunk in which she was imprisoned was pumped full of carbon monoxide. I couldn't help but wonder if she blamed me with her last breath. I felt Noah's eyes on me, judging my reaction.

By now I was close to Noah, and I believed Noah felt genuine affection for me, as much as his emotions would allow. Still, I always had to consider the distinct possibility that if in any way I posed a threat to his spy catching crusade, he wouldn't kill me, but would instead banish me to some isolated shit hole—prison maybe, on trumped up charges—until this entire investigation was over. Since I had no immediate desire to relocate, especially to some backwater federal institution, I knew my response went a long way in reassuring him that I was indeed a team player, an alright guy.

"Did you plan it this way, or is this just how it all came down?"

"Sometimes you have to make battlefield decisions," Noah explained. "Don't second guess this. Our Mystery Man was one of their most promising young men in the Ministry of State Security. He was a brilliant guy, and his parents were pure commie blue blood, came up through the ranks with Mao and the gang. He was educated in Europe and Moscow, and he was trained in his craft in North Korea. He was an expert in many areas. For us, he was a genuine score, a prize worth the risk and worth the consequences."

"Then I'm glad it worked out alright."

Noah nodded in what I was to take for his empathy and understanding. It was all bullshit of course. He had used me, and I went for my personal adrenaline rush in the guise of patriotic duty. Now two people were dead, and I would never know if the gain was truly worth it.

I watched Noah examine the ash on his cigarette, debating on whether to let it keep burning or flick it into the ashtray. He flicked the ash, took one more drag and then stubbed out the butt, before sitting back in his chair.

"The suitcase was pure gold," he assured me, deciding now that we had the downside resolved he would sell me on the pluses. "We found all sorts of cash and credit cards issued to different names. But the main thing was the telephone numbers and list of contacts, agents operating in this country. At a glance, some of the names coincide with Cindy's contacts. Remember her? The Chinese woman you saw that night at Louie's. We've had surveillance all over her, and believe me, she's a popular girl. She's in contact with a lot of very interesting people.

"But now with the suitcase we have corroboration in two places. And the trick with espionage cases, if you remember what I told you, is to nail them with at least two sources. Three ways are better still. We found in that suitcase that their spy operation is very widespread and tough to root out."

"Yeah, but you knew that already."

Noah only shrugged, and I knew it was best to leave it alone, at least for the moment. Judging by the look on his face, I was sure whatever he found in that suitcase was extremely sobering. Noah wasn't playacting. Not this time. I bit my lip and filed away the questions. If I wanted answers, then I would have to continue playing the game. And that was his hook in me, or at least one of them. Knowing what others didn't.

chapter

TWENTY-TWO

On a morning in late November I read in the paper that Larry Wu Tai Chin, a senior member of the CIA was accused of serving as a double agent and spying for China. I started to read the article when the telephone rang. It was Noah.

"You home?"

"You just called me here."

"Put on some coffee."

A half an hour later he was standing at my door. He was smiling like a schoolboy who just got an "A" on his science test.

"I thought you were in Washington."

"Got back this morning. You saw the paper? First Rosner and now Chin."

"Rosner was about spying for Israel."

Noah eyed me like I was a carnival sideshow oddity. "And then some. They caught Rosner and his wife with top-secret documents. It was a package intended for the Chinese. What information we believe he did manage to give them almost blew our whole operation. That sonofabitch!"

"And Mister Chin? What's his story?"

"We tricked him good. Fucker dug his grave with his very own mouth. We showed him the evidence, how we had him dead to rights. He almost filled his drawers. In desperation, he offered to serve as a double agent, this time betraying China on behalf of the United States. We told him; sure, we're interested, as long as you chronicle how you spied for China all these years.

"He sang for six hours. When the music stopped, he was taken into custody.

"Chin went all the way back to the forties, passing them classified documents. Small wonder we had limited success in our operations against them. They always knew how we were playing our cards."

"And the CIA knew nothing about Chin. Not a clue for all this time?"

"Can't win them all," Noah allowed grudgingly.

"It's a big one not to win. A mighty big one to lose. How did you know about Chin?" I found myself asking.

Noah hesitated and then he grunted, weighing the confidential information against the value of the lesson I could learn here.

"You remember the briefcase from our Mystery Man?" he reminded me. "The one I told you was so important?"

I nodded.

"And you remember the man who came and went?"

"You mean Yurchenko," I said, noting the Soviet KGB agent who had allegedly defected to the United States and re-defected back to Russia. "He dropped a dime on them?"

"That's right. And you know what other name popped up in the Mystery Man's suitcase? Cindy. The Chinese woman you first saw at Louie's house that night. We've been on her tail since the night she approached me up at the restaurant. I think one of the reasons he might have come in was to help get her out of the country. She's hot, and she knows it. At least five file boxes worth of activities."

"No shit. You linked her and Chin. And Yurchenko? What about him?"

"Yurchenko gave up Howard and Pelton, a few of their burnouts to make it look like he was only ratting out their Russian moles. But he also blew Chin for us, and he helped tip us to Rosner. Apparently the Russians have known for years that Chin was spying for the Chinese. When the two countries were buddies, they shared their information. Now…well…things have changed."

I smiled. I realized this was one of those frequent times in human events when the reality was one thing, the story another, and the interpretation of that story was the crap you find in the news. By the time every pundit finished putting their spin on it, the entire affair would be so saturated with opinions the public would be numb and apathetic. Hence we have history.

"And Rosner? Was he connected to Chin?"

The smile abruptly left Noah's face. "That no good sonofabitch. They're trying to make him out like some kind of martyr. Like he was some kind of idealist. He took money, for Christ sakes. He sold his soul for a lousy few bucks."

"And he's connected to Chin?" I persisted.

Before I could ask again, Noah fished in his briefcase until he removed a manila envelope. He stared at me for a moment, so I knew by the look in his eyes that he was about to trust me with some very serious information. By now I knew the look, and realized it served partly as a warning not to betray him. By now it was just another accessory to our standard routine. By now he had concluded that my personal principles would never allow me to betray him.

"What I'm about to show you is for your eyes only."

"I understand."

He removed a photo from the envelope and passed it to me. Larry Chin was in the photo, and he was talking to another man. They were standing in a shopping mall somewhere, judging from the surroundings. The other man in the photo was Jeremy Rosner."

"You see that? Talk about right on the money."

"You're sure?"

"China wants to get its hands on certain military technology they can't steal from us, so they were hoping they could obtain it from Israel. We think Chin and Rosner were serving as the intermediaries."

I studied the photo for another minute or so and then slid it back to Noah, who returned it to its envelope.

"The American Jews think it's all about Israel, so no wonder they're all upset. But even the Israelis who were running Rosner probably don't know the full extent of his double dealing with China and maybe Russia and Pakistan. When they recruited him, they created their own monster."

"And you can't go public, claiming there is a lot more involved than just Israel?"

"Hell, no. If we disclosed what we knew, we would be informing the Chinese to what extent Rosner compromised our current investigation. They might start closing operations down, until things blew over. And we would be left in the dark again.

Noah took a drag on his cigarette and slowly got up to leave.

"There is something I need your help with. This should be fun."

"What is it?"

"You know the tracts and the way they are coded? I think I found out who wrote the codes."

I walked Noah to his car and promised to meet him the following afternoon. As he drove off, I thought about Chin and Rosner, and how facts can often be either omitted or compiled in such a way as to either serve or avoid the truth. In this case very little of the truth was ever revealed to the public. Before any facts could leak out, both men were ushered off into oblivion. Chin was found guilty of espionage a few months later. He committed suicide in his cell by wrapping a plastic bag around his face. Rosner was given life without the possibility of parole.

Throughout the end of that year and into the next many more arrests were made. In terms of the media, 1985 would become known as the "Year of the Spy."

chapter

TWENTY-
THREE

Since the time of our initial meetings, Noah Brown had been promising to add an extra room to his house, a lab of sorts where he could invite me inside. My vision of this lab was a pristine structure lit by recessed embankments of fluorescent lights. I envisioned sterility and precision spacing and arrangement, like you would find at Hughes or Honeywell or any of the larger developers of advanced technology. And if that was not to be the case, I expected the kind of decor you would find at Cal Tech or Stanford, or at the very least at some small town junior college.

But Noah's new laboratory, as so it was named, paled by contrast to the majesty of my science lab in junior high school.

Except for the dozen computers that stood in a row on cheap folding tables Noah had reinforced with plywood, there was little order to the austere seven hundred square foot add-on. Tools and parts were lying everywhere, as were thousands of floppy disks, stored in unlabeled plastic cases and scattered about in piles. The concrete floor was bare of anything but dust; save for the times Noah gave a once over with his bristle challenged push broom. The interior walls were bereft the extravagance of drywall, leaving exposed sections of foil wrapped number thirty insulation that were wedged in between the roughly hewn wooden studs and braced along the ceiling.

Oscilloscopes and other scopes were stacked up on cheap metal shelving. And on the far wall, a pile of dusty radio equipment balanced precariously on plywood tiers. If there was anything complimentary to say about Noah's new lab, it was that this raw and haphazard interior setting was in perfect harmony with the exterior trash pile that he called his yard. Nevertheless, Noah was proud of the fact that for all intent and purposes the room was actually finished. To him this was an accomplishment.

"There's about ten million bucks worth of stuff in here," Noah boasted. He pointed to the radio equipment on the cinderblocks and plywood, like a college student's makeshift entertainment center. "About seven million right there, alone."

"You couldn't prove it by me," I told him.

He looked astonished. "I just wanted to get it set up so I could work in here. I'll get it all finished one day," he promised, a little embarrassed by my critique.

Yeah, sure you will, I thought to myself. I didn't have the heart to say it to his face.

"So what did you want to see me about?" I asked.

He smiled. "Did you notice the hubbub next door?" he asked, jerking his thumb in the direction of Louie's.

"I saw cars in the driveway."

"Another big pow wow. There are really pissed at poor old Louie. He had them all enthused over the Nicaraguan invasion, and when it didn't come off, he's the big shit eater."

"Who's over there? There are cars in the driveway that I don't recognize."

"Some of them are the usual suspects. But then there are others. New faces. Better dressed. I think what we're seeing here is a new wave of assholes, a passing of the torch, if you will. This new wave, they've been telling Louie it's time for him to hang it up."

"If they're pissing on Louie, then they must really love you for provoking him. They say anything about our trip up north?"

Noah shook his head. "Not that. But you're right. I am on their shit list."

He beckoned me over toward a tape recorder. "Here, I brought this out for you. Listen to this. It's Burt Blount talking to Louie."

Noah flicked on the recorder, and I listened to a very despairing Louie whine to Blount, "You can't say I fucked up. Remember, he did say there was a chance that they would cancel the invasion."

"I checked with all my sources, and there were no plans for any invasion. Nobody is happy about this, Louis. I'm trying to protect you."

"But why would he lie to me?"

There was dead silence on the line for a good five seconds. "I'll leave you to figure that out," Blount said, finally. "Look, there are only three things you can do. You can sell your house and lay low for a couple of years. You can burn down his house. Or you could dust him. Make up your mind and then do it."

"Yes, sir."

"I'm not kidding, Louis. Make up your mind, before someone makes it up for you."

I listened to the click on the line, and for a few seconds after I still heard Louie breathing hard and maybe even sobbing. The poor guy. He had reached out for the big brass ring on this Nicaraguan thing and snatched a turd ticket to nowhere.

"I'd say there's a group in transition," I offered to Noah.

"That's what it's about over there. They're trying to figure out just what to do. The Chinese nationals are putting pressure on them. More of them are moving in, and more of these guys are being shoved out of the way."

"A declining industry for the old school."

"It gets worse. The twenty-two technology companies that are in holding by the Roberts Trust have sustained some terrible losses. We have only been able to break into the four of the twenty-two, but we have had much better luck on the open seas.

"At first we were able to substitute our cargo containers of trucking and automotive parts and building materials in exchange for their cargo containers of missile parts, area surveillance components and computer surveillance equipment. They were shipping smuggled goods through three different routes. Singapore, Shanghai and Sri Lanka."

"But they got wise?"

"Wise enough. They substituted custom shipping crates for the standard ones they were using. The custom crates are easier to distinguish, to track. So we started waylaying the shipments directly, or we worked through certain gangs for hire. There were a couple of Pier One brawls, and a few of the bad guys simply fell off the earth. That's why they are over at Louie's. Trying to figure out what happened to certain members of their team."

"Anyone else fall off the earth?"

"We lost a few, yeah."

How could this crew be that gullible? I'm sorry, but I just don't get it. They have to know their operations have been compromised."

"You're forgetting something, a key aspect in the Asian mentality."

"Louie's boys aren't Asian."

"Doesn't matter. Their system is. So is the hierarchy. Bottom line, they are afraid of losing face. The chief of one section reports to his hierarchy that his group has been badly compromised and, right away he loses face. Then the chief would have to pass it upstairs, and so on. For them losing face is more than embarrassing, it's total humiliation. It could mean a demotion or worse. They would rather watch it go to hell in a hand basket than admit something was wrong.

"And that's where we have them. It's either their need to save face, or their fear of losing it. Call it what you want, but it's so deeply embedded into their culture they will never overcome it. It's that hive mentality."

I looked out the window and shook my head in wonder.

"So here they are, pondering mysteries of destruction, while picking at peanuts and drinking their beers. And they're talking right into your microphone. How could they not be aware you are bugging them?"

"Easy. They found the bug they were supposed to find. So now they feel secure. Speaking of bugs, I found a couple around here. I freeze them with liquid nitrogen, so by first appearances they don't look tampered with. But their circuits are fried. I think I'm really starting to piss them off."

"They'll make a move on you."

Noah shook his head. "I don't think so. Remember, I'm still a prize if they can turn me. Which reminds me; I keep getting calls from these Chinese computer places. They keep offering me work. We're going to have to visit a few, and see what they want me to do. You up for that?"

"Sure. Is that why you asked me here?"

Noah grinned and shook his head, no. "I think I identified the guy who created their cryptic codes. Like I told you, the codes are embedded in the religious tracts, and the religious tracts are the scratch pads they rotate periodically.

"What I didn't tell you was that ever since our visit up north we've been using NORAD, our satellites, helicopters and spy planes to track the orbital route of the Chinese satellites and any ground stations. We think they have been using ground stations to communicate with the satellites by using burst transmissions."

"I thought they transmit from the consulate."

"They do. But they would never put their eggs in one basket. For one thing, it's not very Chinese. They would want to communicate from a number of places. Do you understand what I'm explaining to you?"

"Yeah, I get it. Different sources collect the information and then transmit to the ground stations that beam it up to the satellites."

He nodded, satisfied. "A month or so ago, a courier left an envelope in Louie's mailbox. From time to time we've intercepted these envelopes and either copied the contents and let them go through, or kept them. One had some information about Hawaii along with a ticket to the Big Island. Sure enough, we found they were transmitting from a mountain facility. We sent someone in there, posing as a retired industrialist who had turned into a spiritual nut. That's after we found the ground station attendant browsing the New Age bookstore."

"I suppose they are buddies now."

"Count on it. Our guy tells the bad guy he has studied advanced meditation for many years and is searching for ways to leave his body."

"He should try the grass over there. That's a good first step to leaving your body."

"C'mon, be serious here for a minute."

"Okay, I'm serious."

"We found other stations in the mountains in upstate New York and in Colorado, which makes sense, since we found Chinese satellites fly over those places on a regular basis.

"Oh. Not all places are hooked up to the satellites. We figure the Denver station hooks up with New Orleans through ground communications, somehow, since the satellites don't fly over New Orleans."

"What about California?"

"We still haven't found it."

"And the codes?"

Noah reached around into a shelf and pulled out a dog-eared book. "Look at this," he said, handing it to me.

I read the cover—Innovations in Computer Communication, by Roger Song. "This is it?"

Noah nodded. "Uh huh, that's our boy. I remembered Song from back in the sixties, when he was trying to peddle his own security system. He had been working for the Navy and a few other government science agencies, as well as one of the larger commercial research labs. He was no lightweight. Just to be sure I had the right guy, I went looking back through all the old science conference rosters that I had attended in different cities. Song kept coming up in the register. I knew we had a match."

"So where did you find this?" I asked, holding up the book.

"I told you I never throw anything out."

"And Song? Where is he now?"

"That's what's so funny. Song thought his encryption was foolproof. It's based loosely on how the Chinese record the phases of the moon. But his encryption has its vulnerabilities. That's the reason he never sold it."

"But he did sell it, or he gave it away. To the Chinese."

"Yep. And now they're going to rue the day. I used Song's code and broke the religious tracts. I got them now. I whipped the fucker at his own damn game."

"So soon you'll be able to intercept the transmissions?"

"It's not that easy," Noah lamented. "From what we are getting, the Chinese satellites have a ninety minute presence, approximately. They fly high over the United States and low over China. It will be hard to intercept their burst transmissions, since the frequencies are very narrow. We would have to be within three hundred feet of the transmission site. We'll try it first with helicopters, and if that doesn't work, we'll have to work it from the ground."

"But you can do it?"

"We may have to locate their satellite stations. Break them down and study their transmission process. That could take awhile. But meanwhile, I'm going to teach a class at the University, and you will be among my students. I convinced a professor friend of mine that he should call in sick for a couple of weeks, and I will sub his class."

"Do you have any idea how much I hated school?"

"Song is teaching there. He is an assistant professor. I want to bug the bastard and tie him even further to the group. I also want to see who else on campus is in his club."

A few nights later Noah began teaching class at UCLA, and I was his dumbest student. The subject he taught was Sub-Orbital Mathematics, and it was a safe guess that I was the only one in the room who didn't have a clue what he was talking about. So I sat there, sometimes with pen in hand, pretending to take notes on what to me was a foreign language. Now and then I would wrinkle my brow and rub my chin, as if the very profundity of the subject matter was impacting the far reaches of my brain. I suppose the class was God's little joke for a committed clock watcher and academic underachiever.

My eyes were practically dedicated to the passage of time as recorded by that slow moving bastard of a clock above the classroom door. Two days into the class, I was subscribing avidly to the allegedly French saying that the more things change the more they stay the same. School was boring.

But after three nights of calling off our operation, as Noah liked to call it, we finally found the perfect opportunity to bug Song's classroom. Noah had the key, so the coming and going was pretty easy. We inserted one listening device under his desk and another inside the heating unit. We also bugged his phone. A few minutes later we were gone.

Song's office, however, was an entirely different story. Noah quite rightly believed bugs planted there were to our best advantage since the odds were any confidential conversations, in person or over the telephone, would be conducted in Song's office and not his classroom. The problem was, unlike the classroom, some of the instructors would often stay late, working on their students' tests and papers, or sitting around shooting the shit. Song was among them, holding court with three other Chinese colleagues who also taught in that department. Besides Song, there was one professor in the office next door to Song's—an Anglo who Noah learned was going through a bitter divorce. Rather than go home or to the presumably lonely bachelor apartment he now occupied, the man stayed and drank in his office until after midnight.

The cleaning crews presented an added problem, as did the security that made the office rounds more frequently than they examined the classrooms. So while it was hardly like breaking into Fort Knox, it wasn't nearly as easy a task as bugging the classrooms. If we screwed it up, we risked the embarrassment of getting caught, plus the ever present danger of tipping the Chinese to the extent of the overall investigation. Exposure could compromise the efforts of hundreds of federal agents.

Time passed as we waited for our chance. And awaiting our chance meant more time in school. More time in school meant that a few of the actual students in Noah's class now found me more familiar, and they would approach me, discussing the evening's lesson. I did more than my share of nodding and agreeing, and every now and then I ventured those tidbits from the lecture that I had retained.

"If we don't crack his office pretty soon," I'll have to start cutting your class."

"Remember, it's for your country," he said, whipping out that chestnut and another round of sentiment.

Before I was discovered as a science fraud, Noah and I finally found the opportunity to bug Song's office. Noah had a key and access to his friend's office, the professor for whom he was subbing, and we had started using that office on a regular basis, so that security and the other instructors would be familiar with us. After a week of establishing our routine, one night we discovered the floor was empty and the offices dark, save for the office next to Song's, the one belonging to the newly divorced Anglo professor.

"What now?"

"Fuck it. Let's do it. If he decides to come in, we'll just have to knock him out."

"No good. He's a professor, not a terrorist."

"So what then?"

I thought and searched, and then it came to me. "I know. "Connie."

"Who, what?"

"She lives nearby, and if she's home she can be over here in fifteen minutes. She owes me favors, but you'd still better give her a couple hundred."

"Who is Connie?"

"A hooker. She'll have the divorced guy hearing bells and not us."

At first Noah looked perplexed, and then he got it. I watched his eyes light up, and then the hopeful look that maybe later he could play with Connie.

"A couple of hundred?"

"Hey, it's for your country," I threw back in his face. "Are we going or not?"

"Yeah, do it. You sure she'll come?"

By then I had dialed and had Connie on the phone. She was no ordinary prostitute; she was someone I had known for years. She was the former longtime lover of a very close friend of mine. Despite all our history, Connie and I had never consummated much more than a few drinks. During the past six months, she had put on a few pounds and was thinking of retirement. It was hooker talk for growing bored and losing business. But if nothing else, Connie was a clutch player, and the poor divorcing professor at the other end of the hall, well he didn't stand a chance.

Good to her word, twenty minutes later I found Connie peeking through our office door. She was wearing a dark red wig.

"I wasn't sure this was the right place," she laughed. "It's confusing around here, anymore, with all these new buildings."

"You have been here before?" Noah asked in surprise, as Connie crossed the floor to kiss me hello in her two story platform shoes. Despite the cold weather, she wore satin shorts that began and ended at the seam of her crotch, a faux fur coat, a silk shell with no bra and jewelry.

"Yeah, I went here for a couple of years. Hard to believe, isn't it?" she laughed.

Noah looked surprised she was reading his thoughts. I knew from previous conversations that Noah had little personal experience with hookers, and clearly Connie intrigued him. If nothing else, Connie wasn't stupid.

"Noah has money for you," I gestured, pulling Noah from his fantasies.

He glanced at me sternly and reluctantly pulled two hundred dollar bills from his wallet. Once she tucked the money into her handbag, Connie started to take off her clothes.

"No, it's not him," I told her, much to Noah's increasing disappointment. "There's a guy down the hall. He's going through a messy divorce. So make him happy, and, above all, keep him distracted for a good thirty minutes or so. I don't want him paying attention to anything but you."

Connie smiled. "Like he really has a chance."

"And needless to say, this stays in this room."

"Gotcha."

I opened the door and pointed. Connie strolled down the hallway on her platform shoes and stopped in front of the professor's office. Pausing briefly at the professor's door, Connie checked her lipstick and fussed with her wig, and then she walked into his life.

A few minutes later Noah and I were inside Song's office. Not too long after that, we had bugs in his phone, inside the lamp on his desk, as well as the lamp where visitors sat.

"These send strong signals," Noah assured me. "They'll pick up anything that's said in the room."

As if on cue, from the office next door we began to hear a lot of moaning and slamming. The professor's desk chair was subjecting itself to terrible abuse as it smacked against the chalkboard. I doubted if the professor cared at all about his chair, having surrendered himself to Connie's charms.

"Pretty physical," Noah assessed with unabashed approval as he copied files off of Song's computer onto floppy disks. "Will you give me her number?"

Next door the sighs and moans, the body slamming was getting louder. Something heavy, a book maybe, fell to the floor.

The ivory tower was being shaken to its core. Noah shook his head at me, a man perplexed by the machinations of the post-modern world.

"Are we almost through here?" I asked, getting his mind off his dick.

"You know, she could do a lot worse than spend some time with me."

"Yeah, sure. You'd want to reform her, or start probing into her personal life, asking all sorts of ridiculous questions. You're just that kind."

Once we were finished, we wiped carefully for our finger-prints and slipped out the door, closing it behind us. The sounds of sex were louder now, as Connie and the professor entered the second round.

I glanced through the window. Connie was astride the pro-fessor, and it struck me funny to see his decade old, funky cordu-roy pants pulled down around his scuffed Rockport shoes.

"Maybe I'd better break this up."

"You're cruel, even crueler than I am."

I nodded. "Alright. I'll talk to her later. School is out. Let's get something to eat."

chapter

TWENTY-
FOUR

On the way to Noah's house he was still asking me about Connie, and I took the opportunity to tease him unmercifully.

"That was real smart," Noah conceded as a more sober assessment. "It was a battlefield decision."

"Is that what it was?" I laughed. "Then a medal should be forthcoming. The Purple Penis."

I had grown accustomed to leaving my car at Noah's house so we could drive to the university together. Typically, we would go for dinner after, and then we would return to his house where, depending on the hour, we would either kick around new information or I would simply get in my car and drive home. It was well after midnight when we returned to his house. Noah pulled in and parked the Corvette near the El Camino and the other vehicles that were part of his collection. I was tired and distracted, not paying much attention to our surroundings. I got out of the car and went to help Noah out of the driver's side when I heard what I thought was a footstep on a stray sheet of metal strewn around the yard.

I no sooner turned my head than a sneakered figure came bolting out of the shadows. I was startled at first, frightened, but out of sheer reflex I went low and threw a cross body block, catching the guy's knees in my ribs. The man stumbled and staggered on scraps in the yard, bouncing off the Corvette's fender. It was only then I saw the knife in the man's hand.

Without hesitation, Noah Brown was on him, hobbling after his prey like an angry crab. I was amazed how quickly he could move on those withered, crippled legs. Noah grabbed the man's jacket with one hand, and with the other he issued a picture perfect karate chop against the carotid artery. The man gasped a few times, and abruptly the gasping stopped. The man went limp.

"Is he dead?"

"I would think so," Noah declared phlegmatically.

"Did you have to kill him?"

Noah was genuinely offended. "This one tried to kill me. This should send a message that they better stay the fuck off of my property."

My ribs hurt. I was in no mood to argue.

"Look at him," Noah gestured. "Chinese. Could be someone tracking us down from our odyssey in Northern California. We'd better get rid of the body."

I stared down at the man, still waiting for him to move. It wasn't about to happen.

"So what do we do? Do you call someone to get him vacuumed up, or what?"

"Not on this case. It's you and me. You up for a little digging?"

I rubbed the pain in my side where the dead man's knee had caught me. "It wasn't what I had planned."

"Break anything?"

"Don't think so," I answered, trying not to grimace.

"Just ribs."

Noah grabbed the dead man's shoulders. "Here, get his legs."

I watched Noah in silent admiration. I was simply amazed how, when the occasion called for it, Noah could summon the strength and balance that appeared beyond the capacity of his crippled body. A couple of moments earlier, I was helping him out of his car. Now he was ready to dig a grave.

"Are you helping me, or not?"

If I had to speculate, I would have expected a wave of misgivings to wash over me. I would have thought the fear of consequence and the outright creepiness of transporting and burying a dead man would have given me sufficient pause. But when the moment came, I was able to dispel those misgivings. I grabbed the legs, and together Noah and I slung the dead man into the bed of the El Camino and covered him with canvas tarp.

I stood listening to the coyotes howl, staring at the sky while Noah rummaged around the yard for a pick and a couple of shovels. I watched him charge inside the house, emerging several minutes later with two pairs of boots, work gloves and coveralls. It was going to be a long night.

"Where is Louie and his body dumping boat, now that we need him?" Noah joked as we climbed inside the cab of the El Camino.

"Where are we taking him?"

"To the desert."

An couple hours out of town, we turned off the Interstate onto a state road and, finally, onto a dirt road that seemed to lead into the middle of nowhere.

"Do you know where we're going?" I asked, hoping we weren't searching randomly for just the right burial plot.

"I supervised the installation of military antennas back through here," Noah assured me. "I know these roads by heart."

Sure enough, Noah didn't miss a trick as we drove for maybe ten miles down the dirt road. I was relieved when he finally pulled over and parked. I had to pee so badly I could barely stand it. When I did pee, the sound of the streaming urine hitting the sandy soil reverberated inside my head like water over the Hoover Dam. I thought the entire world would be drawn out by the noise to witness a crippled old killer and a dead man waiting for me to put my dick back in my fly.

Digging through that soil was no easy task, and it took us the better part of a half hour to dig a grave three to four feet deep. I was grateful Noah had brought the pick to break up the crusty top layer of sun dried sand and soil. The gloves also came in handy. If nothing else, Noah knew what it took to bury a body.

"You sure that's enough?" I said, examining the hole.

"Yeah, that's enough. Let's go get him."

I was the first to arrive at the El Camino. I jumped inside the bed and dragged the body so that his head and shoulders were dangling over the side of the truck bed just off the ground. I was about to give the body a final shove out of the bed when I felt something jerk under me. Not sure whether it really happened or not, I kicked lightly at the body, and I felt it twitch. Seconds later, I heard it moan, and I shivered involuntarily.

"He's still alive, I think," I whispered, feeling the cold chill of revelation ride the subway from my heart to testicles.

"Let me see," offered Noah, pressing his face closer in search of signs of life.

It looked for a minute like he was coming to his rescue, the way Noah listened for breathing and tapped the ailing Chinese, causing him to twitch and moan again. I was wrong. Without hesitation, Noah brought the blade of his hand down across the man's throat, crushing his larynx. The man jerked and twitched a couple of times, wheezing desperately. His revival was over. He was a body again. But just to be sure, Noah grabbed the chin and hair and snapped its neck.

"You want to drown him, just in case?"

"No water. It's the desert."

I stared down at the body of the Chinese operative. His eyes were open, staring up at the sky. I wondered if in his life he had ever given a second's consideration to dying in America, to being buried thousands of miles from his home. Then again, the guy could have just as easily come from Monterey Park or West Covina as Mainland China. Who was to know? Someone. Someone would realize he was missing and come looking for him. Of that we could be certain.

We buried the body just as the sky was turning from black to the first shades of pre-dawn gray. I had seen the sky that color on many occasions, most of them after staying up the better part of the night, clubbing it with friends, or returning home from an amorous tryst. I had been out many dozens of nights that turned into mornings, when the sun started to rise and the streetlights switched off in a brief but always surprising moment of magic. But this late night funeral session gave that time an entirely different spin.

From then on, every time I saw the desert shifting in the moonlight I would wonder if someone was buried beneath that very spot I was staring at. Among its many purposes, the desert was a repository for the artifacts of personal human struggle. Forever changing and telling no tales.

chapter

TWENTY-FIVE

It was just around the time that Larry Chin was first arrested that then FBI Director William H Webster initiated a media campaign designed to make the American public aware of rampant spying within these shores.

"FBI Chief Puts Stress on Catching Foreign Spies," read the Los Angeles Times. A few weeks later, another headline read "Pattern of China Links Emerging in Spy Cases, Intelligence Experts Say That Door Opened to Peking Also Invites Espionage Risk." A few days later another headline read, "Senate Votes to Delay China Nuclear Accord, Moves to Block Sales Until Reagan Certifies Non-Proliferation Safeguards are Adequate."

Meanwhile, despite all the public controversy about spying and China, Noah was receiving steady calls from all over the country. The calls came from Chinese technology companies, requesting his services. If Louie and his group couldn't snatch the prize, then someone else would get it done.

Sometimes I went with Noah, and just as often he would travel alone to the aging bedroom communities of Los Angeles where Asian immigrants had recently settled. Most of the Chinese industrial and technological facilities were located in this area, usually occupying spaces in strip malls or recently constructed industrial parks.

One place seemed like the next to me, and in fact they were often connected. Although smiling Chinese gentlemen fronted each individual business with names like Sun Wu and Walter Long, it became clear over time that nearly all these seemingly independent enterprises were part of the commercial operations controlled by the People's Liberation Army.

At each place we visited, the supposed owner posed to Noah the same series of problems. The main complaint, I discovered was the computers they were importing from China were deemed dangerous and produced far too much radiation to pass the standards established by the FCC.

"You work for government? You can help get approval from the FCC?"

The routine became pretty standard with each place that Noah visited. He would promise to help them, and dutifully asked for a nominal advance payment. The company would cut him a check, and federal agents would use the check to establish a paper trail. Later, members of the federal task force, now numbering in the hundreds of agents, would break into these Chinese establishments in search of the incriminating paper trail.

Through covert activities they would determine how this company or that one was ultimately linked together.

"All roads lead to China," Noah pronounced while setting out on his laboratory table samples of boxes, labels and stationary from suspect technological companies.

"Look at all this," he gestured. "All the companies have similar brochures. The invoices, and even the shipping boxes, they are all uniform. One company is the same as the next. The businesses may have different names, but at the end of the day there is only one true company. The PLA. The People's Liberation Army.

I nodded. "No matter. We're talking major micro and macro-management here."

"You have to remember—China is still a warlord operation. Only in the modern world, one warlord controls the cheap labor for tool production, this one the small weapons, and this guy the sneaker manufacturing. Back somewhere in China sits the big warlord of computers, and here in the states all these generals run the field operations."

I was about to question Noah further when a figure appeared in the doorway. It was Louie, wearing a button down oxford and regimental tie, a clean pair of corduroys, and shoes that were shined half-heartedly.

"Hi guys," he greeted nervously.

We eyeballed the boxes spread across the table, fearing any effort to conceal them would only arouse Louie's suspicions. I watched his face for any sign he recognized the labels on the boxes.

"Well look what the cat dragged in," bellowed Noah. "Where the hell have you been? You're supposed to be the head of the neighborhood watch, and you're hardly around anymore. No wonder the thieves are robbing us blind."

"You got robbed?" Louie exclaimed, unable to hide his surprise.

"Somebody is always taking something out of the yard. I lose more tools out there."

By insinuation, Noah was accusing Louie, but Louie tried to ignore it.

"How have you been, Louie?"

"Okay," he responded half-heartedly. "What about you?"

"Noah and I have been writing down his war stories," I lied, since that was our going cover. We were working on a book about Noah's exploits in the Second World War.

"Can I read anything?"

"No," we answered in unison.

"Well give me a copy when it's published."

"Sure will."

Louie hesitated as he determined the best way to unburden himself of the weight on his mind.

"I decided I'm selling my practice," he announced. "It's a good time, and I've been offered good money. And besides, they discovered I may have a touch of Parkinson's Disease."

"Oh shit! You're kidding me?"

"That's too bad. You've seen a doctor?"

"Yeah," Louie nodded.

I watched him lower his head, and I noticed that Noah and I, despite all of Louie's treachery, couldn't help but feel compassion and sympathy for Louie. Maybe it was something in Louie's personality, the good guy quality that would emerge from behind the deceit and psychosis, which elicited from us a genuine sense of caring.

"What are you planning on doing?" Noah asked him.

"I've been taking real estate courses. I'll go for my license pretty soon."

"That's good. It beats waving that gun around."

"And I'm selling the house."

"You are?"

Louie nodded and looked away. I sensed it wasn't entirely his decision.

"It's time to move on. Someone is offering me close to a million for the property, so hey, I'm out of here."

"Where will you go?"

"Looks like you guys have been shopping," said Louie, taking note of the boxes. "New computers?"

"Naw," protested Noah, grabbing a box and turning it upside down. He shook it for added effect and a few pieces of paper fell out and covered the floor. "We've been collecting some of this crap and storing it away."

"So, where are you moving?" I asked again.

"My friend, Daryl, has a condo in Newport Beach. I might move in with him for a while, until I find a place I want to buy. Daryl is into sailing, so maybe I can do a little of that. See how I like it."

"You just want to attract the cuties," Noah joked. "You'll never give up chasing the babes."

Louie blushed, grateful for the accusation. "Well, I just thought I'd tell you," he said, and then, reluctantly, he shuffled off toward his house.

"He wanted to stay and hang out," I said to Noah, after Louie was gone.

"He misses us. He misses you. Especially now that his own people are pushing him out."

"You think that's what's happening?"

"I'm sure of it," Noah acknowledged, gesturing toward the tape recorder. "I snookered him, and some of his cronies are really pissed off. The Bishop won't talk to him. The last time Louie telephoned, the Bishop told him, 'It's advisable you don't call here anymore'."

"That's fucked up. With all the Chinese Nationals coming into the country and taking charge of the network, I guess they're putting him out to pasture."

"You know the Chinese venerate their elderly, so they try to recycle them into meaningful places in society. In this case it backfired on them."

"Maybe. But the boxes sure weren't lost on him. I was watching his eyes."

"Yeah, I know. If we're lucky, the people he'll call will pass it off as another Louie hyperbole. If we're not...well, we'll find out soon enough."

I nodded, wondering if this was the opportune time to be asking a question that had haunted me for months. "You once told me Louie's first lapse into catatonia was a result of something he did as a kid."

"He was a teenager, yeah. It was the first time we know about that he lashed out in fury. Then he sat in a padded room of a couple of years. He didn't talk, he seldom moved. He just stared at the wall in silence."

"What did he do?" I asked. "Did you ever find out what set him off?"

Noah smiled disdainfully at the suggestion he had failed to gain such vital information. He looked at me like I should have known better and abruptly the smile left his face. He leaned forward in his chair and spoke in a barely audible whisper, as if he were afraid someone was listening in.

"He killed his father."

The shock of it caught me off guard. I looked at Noah for reassurance that I had heard him correctly. He was nodding at me.

"Put four bullets into his old man. That's how it all started."

chapter

TWENTY-SIX

A week after Louie announced he was selling his house and moving away, Noah received a mysterious phone call from a woman with a high, squeaky voice who was asking that he meet with her later that night in a restaurant in Monterey Park.

"I have a business proposition for you," she told him in broken English. "I'll give you information for a favor."

I saw he was shaken as after he hung up the phone.

"This is no good," he muttered more to himself than to me.

"It's the boxes. Somebody bought Louie's story."

"It's a set up. I know it, and so do you."

"Are you coming with me?"

I swallowed my fear. "I can't leave you hanging."

"You don't have to, you know."

"Fuck you."

He smiled. "A few good years, and you'll be crazier than I am."

"I'm not sure I'm looking forward to that."

He nodded, sighing. "Believe me, I'll understand."

Less than an hour later we were in standing in an empty strip mall in Monterey Park, one in a series of contiguous communities that rambled east of Pasadena and south of the foothills of the San Gabriel Mountains. The majority of the population was Asian and more specifically of Chinese descent, so it was no surprise the main boulevards were lined with Chinese restaurants and retail and service shops with the business signs written in Chinese as well as English.

"This isn't good," sighed Noah.

"Why did they lead us here, to an empty strip mall? It's too public for a hit."

"They're watching us. I can feel the hairs rising on the back of my neck. Let's get the hell out of here."

We didn't say much else to each other as we drove toward home, getting off the freeway at Van Nuys Boulevard. It had started to drizzle, and the empty streets were wet and slippery. We ascended Beverly Glen into the Santa Monica Mountains, leading to the top of Beverly Hills. We were still on the straightaway when I saw Noah's head jerk suddenly as he glanced into his rearview mirror.

I turned around in my seat and spotted a newer model Volkswagen Cabriolet following behind us. We were the only two cars on the road.

"Better hold on!" Noah shouted as he tromped on the gas.

The Corvette roared to life and skidded momentarily on the slippery asphalt, until it rediscovered its traction and roared up the hill. Noah was still fiddling with the side view mirror when I saw the first two flashes. Noah cursed once and downshifted, and soon we were putting greater distance between the Volkswagen and us. Three more gunshots flashed out of the Volkswagen, and I heard bullets scratch at the top of the roof.

We reached the crest of the mountain, where Beverly Glen crossed over Mulholland, and found a red traffic light waiting at the intersection. Noah ignored it, blasting on through at ninety miles an hour as we began our descent toward the city side of the hills. We were maybe halfway to Sunset Boulevard when Noah slowed the car and pulled into a tiny storefront parking lot. He killed the lights and waited. Until then, we hadn't said a word to each other.

"I think he turned off at Mulholland," Noah speculated, breaking our silence.

He showed me his left arm. "Look at this."

There were four small holes in his upper arm—two were entrance wounds and two where the bullets had taken their leave. Thin and jagged rivulets of blood trickled from each of the holes.

"Shit."

"At least they're clean wounds. I'll be okay, unless he poisoned the bullets. Here, throw me that towel in the back," he gestured.

I handed him the towel, which he wrapped around his arm.

"I'm going to have to see a doctor."

"You want me to drive?"

He considered, and then he nodded reluctantly. I came around to his side and helped him out of his car. By then he had pulled his nine-millimeter pistol from its storage compartment, and he held it in his hand.

"He could be waiting for us back at my house. You'd better be ready."

I drove back to his house, and we found no one there. I waited inside the lab and sipped coffee while Laura, Noah's housekeeper, applied fresh dressings to the wounds. I determined by her calm that she had been through this before. Thirty minutes later the doctor arrived, carrying his black medical bag. The doctor and Noah were quite familiar with each other, either colleagues or friends, or both.

I sat in relative silence while the two men made small talk as the doctor cleaned the wounds to prevent infection and then stitched up each of the holes. As I watched, the lyrics from Life in the Fast Line, the Eagles hit song, kept flashing through my mind—"The doctor said he's coming, but you got to pay him cash." Well here we were. Welcome to the Hotel California.

"Bastard ruined my jacket," Noah lamented. "It cost me five hundred bucks."

"I know a tailor whose specialty is invisible reweaving," I offered.

"How much?"

"It ain't cheap."

"Damn."

I watched as Noah reflected on the events that left him here. His anger was catching up with his discipline, and now he was starting to steam.

"Did you see him?"

I shook my head, no. "Only the gunshot flashes."

"He was Chinese."

I glanced over at the doctor, who was pretending to ignore the exchange.

"Go ahead," Noah encouraged. "The Doc here has a terrible memory."

I watched the doctor smile as he continued to sew up the wounds.

"Maybe they're upset about our sojourn up north? Maybe it's retribution for their losses and grievances."

I was being obscure, but by this point Noah and I could communicate well through the use of abstractions and obscurities.

"Vengeance for the Mystery Man? It's possible."

"But you're not buying it."

"Not yet. It could be a whole new group. Someone new may have come upon the scene. The group that didn't read the office memo, the one claiming I was desirable and not expendable. A group with its own agenda, its own set of rules."

"So that would put them in competition with Louie and the Loonies, and our basic friendly Chinese."

Noah smiled and fished for a cigarette. He looked at the doctor who was just finishing up.

"Those things will kill you," said the doctor, trying to make a joke. In spite of Noah's assurances, I could see the Doc believed he was into something way over his head. He removed from his bag a bottle of antibiotics and handed them to Noah.

"You'd better take these. Change the wounds twice a day. Unless you need me beforehand, you can come to my office the day after tomorrow."

Noah put on display his newly bandaged arm. He held it like a badge of honor. "Good thing they were only .22's, eh Doc? Not like the last time."

The doctor nodded, but I don't believe he found the size of the bullets of much consolation.

"Good night, Noah," he said. He nodded to me and then Laura escorted him to his car.

"I would really like to get that bastard," Noah declared, shortly after the Doc was gone. "But I can tell you already, it's a rented car leased with phony ID. We won't find any fingerprints."

"You're just lucky he didn't put one in your head. I think that was the intention."

"That little bird on my shoulder," Noah assured me, wagging his finger. "He never lets me down."

"It would have been even better if the bird had shot back at him."

Noah shook his head and studied the ash on his cigarette. "You had better get going. I have to make some calls."

I realized they were the calls no one could overhear, and I stood up and prepared to leave.

"I'll walk you out," he offered, struggling out of his chair.

"That's okay."

"No, really," he said, snatching his pistol off the nearby table. "Just in case."

Out in his yard all was quiet. The misty rain had stopped, and the canyon smelled fresh and clean. Down below the city glistened, and it felt for a moment like nothing had happened. I walked over and inspected Noah's Corvette that was parked underneath the security lights. I saw blood on the exterior part of the door, and on the upholstery.

"Just had it waxed and detailed," Noah sighed, coming up behind me. "It's always tough getting the blood out."

I walked around the car until I noticed that there were two dark and straight parallel lines running across the roofline from the rear window to the windshield. It didn't take much to realize that they were bullet streaks, leaving trails like two torpedoes that had skimmed across the wet surface of the Corvette's roof.

"Take a look at this," I gestured to Noah.

He inspected them carefully. "I guess it's a good thing I had my car waxed, this week. If it was dry night, and the car hadn't been waxed recently, those two bullets might have penetrated the roof and paid us a visit."

"There were five shots in all. Two went into you. Two skimmed across the roof. And the other one?"

Noah shrugged it off. "Who knows? That's why they say every day is a good day when you can spend it above the ground."

chapter

TWENTY-SEVEN

It didn't take nearly as long as I imagined it would for Noah's arm to heal. In a little more than a week the heavy gauze dressings had come off and oversized Band-Aids now covered the wounds. Noah complained his arm was stiff, but that was to be expected. Even the perforated gray tweed sport coat Noah coveted had returned from the tailors, the invisible reweaving a notable success.

We learned from his tapped telephone lines that the Bishop had come down with cancer of the colon. Neither one of us thought the Bishop's inevitable demise would be a tragic loss, but nevertheless we monitored his progress with the interest of greedy relatives. Rather than send him home, Noah had encouraged the administrators to keep the Bishop in the hospital for as long as they could.

"While he is there, federal agents have been going through his house, making copies of everything they can. We have a team of agents, posing as nurses, watching over him in his hospital room. When anyone comes to visit him, they record the conversation. Besides, this way we always know where he is."

"Do many actually dare come to visit him?"

"Louie did once. And that visit didn't exactly cheer up the Bishop. There have been a few clerics from the Old Holy Church, maybe a couple of others. I think a few of the boys suspect the jig is up, their covers are blown, and they are heading out for parts unknown. We try to keep track of them, but we have only so many agents we can deploy."

"Like Louie. He's running."

"He was told to. Louie went for his real estate license the other day, and he passed it. So did the federal agent who was assigned to keep an eye on him. I suppose it'll give him another vocation when he retires from the Bureau.

"Oh, I didn't tell you this," Noah smiled relishing both the story and the fresh cup of coffee that Laura had just served him. "The U.S. Attorney has been so inundated with the workload that he has been getting home late. His suspicious wife, naturally, assumed he was having an affair and was getting ready to leave him. The poor guy practically begged me to visit with his wife and explain to her that he was not having an affair; he was on special assignment and doing his duty like a loyal American.

"The absurdity of war," I said.

"No fooling. It's always remarkable the little things you remember later, along with the big events."

I nodded in agreement. "Probably because the little stuff is so human and more accessible."

Noah nodded and stared into his coffee cup as he weighed how much he should tell me. "We found Blount," he announced, a more somber tone to his voice.

"Burt Blount? I remember when he went driving out from Louie's. I thought agents were on his tail."

"There are only so many agents, and there are increasingly bigger fish to fry. The thing with Blount is he led us to a whole new problem we'll be facing sooner or later. It is a domestic issue."

I sat up, taking notice of the look on Noah's face. He was genuinely worried.

"After we lost him, we put out an APB on Blount. I never did trust the bastard, especially since we know he holds a rank above Louie. Anyway, local sheriffs found him down in Georgia. Blount is installing a fiber optic secure communication system for some right wing nut group. So far, he has run it for fourteen miles, and then he spliced it into an old railroad line for another twenty-two miles, and then out again.

"The group boasts about two hundred persons, and women and children are allowed to enter the premises. At first we thought it might be the Klan, but it's not. Definitely not. It's something new on the horizon. It calls itself a militia formed by traditional patriots, or some such nonsense. I never dreamed I would see so many nut cases walking around this country."

Noah paused and shook his head. "One day the toilet will flush. It's a matter of time. A ton of crap will be flushed down the toilet."

I didn't think so. I was getting the hint we were engaged in what was ultimately a losing battle. Chalk it up to too little too late. Chalk it up to the confluence of events and the changing of the times. But to me it did not bode well. I thought of the book Noah liked to tout so much, "Lessons of History," by Will and Ariel Durant. Oddly, perhaps, Noah had been friends with them and held a special place in his heart for the now deceased couple who had contributed so much in letters, history, and philosophy. I thought about one of my personal favorites, "Revolt of the Masses," by Ortega Y Gassett, and I considered Rome and other empires and their ignominious declines. I realized the dumbed down knuckleheads had a greater chance of overwhelming civilization than of being flushed away by the remaining guardians of culture and civilization, whoever they were. But I wasn't about to tell that to Noah. After all those decades of his fending the Barbarians from our gates, he didn't need to hear my dark prognosis for his legacy.

"If Blount is installing fiber optics for them, it's costing a few bucks," I offered instead. "Somebody with clout has to be backing that play."

"We're looking, believe me. We're looking hard."

"I thought you couldn't bug secure fiber optics communications."

A grin swept in over Noah's worried face. "We sure hope they believe that."

Abruptly the grin left his face, and he turned serious. "There is something I have to tell you."

"Obviously, it is something I don't want to hear."

"All the press releases about Chinese espionage operations are starting to make certain people uncomfortable. You know the book, Captains and Kings?"

I nodded. "Taylor Caldwell."

"Well this is this is the modern, updated version. The Captains and Kings are getting nervous that all this flack about Chinese spying will diminish economic opportunities in Mainland China. They pressure the legislators and the State Department, and they in turn are putting the arm on us."

"You're saying they want you to back off?"

"Somewhat. What they are refusing to acknowledge is either we crack down upon them now, or they scramble and get away. And then they set up shop someplace else and do it all over again. Only then it's a newer system with newer faces, and we'll be forced to start from scratch."

"I thought it was determined these Chinese operations posed a clear danger to the American public."

"It was, and they do. But the big bucks talk, and everything else ceases to become a priority. It sounds crazy, I know, but more than a few believe we can allow a few transgressions for a larger piece of the market share."

"It's logical. As long as neither country decides to break it off. Or go to war. So what do you do?"

"Oh, I don't stop. I keep chasing it down. We do as much damage to their operations as we possibly can, until someone orders us to turn it off. Remember the game? Beat the Clock? Well, this is Beat the Clock."

I studied Noah's face and saw he was embarrassed and for good reason. To get me aboard he had blown the bugle and beat the war drum, and did some serious cheerleading for the Intelligence, Defense and even the Justice communities. And while there was still some truth in his glorification, the undercoating of fearful and subservient bureaucrats was beginning to eat through the fragile, romantic patina of dedication and sacrifice. As always, commerce, if not greed itself, would prevail.

"So you are acquiescing to the theory that engagement with China will result in greater benefits and economic opportunities?"

"What the hell do you want me to do?" He was clearly frustrated by it all. "Maybe so. I don't know at this point," he admitted, surprising himself as well as me. "History dictates otherwise," he offered in balance.

I shrugged. "Not much you can do. Time moves on. Maybe it is time to make money and not war. Soon enough, China will dominate Asia and have a stronger influence in the rest of the world. From what you say, and from what I see, it looks now as that is unavoidable. You can view it as opportunity. Most will. Or you can see it as being fucked."

Noah glared at me at first uncertain if I was merely taunting him. "What are you saying, exactly?"

"I'm saying, maybe time has moved on. The traitors are one thing, but the world economy is quite another. China will be a great power, and we'll have to learn to deal with it. The Age of Steam is upon us."

He grunted, considering, coming to grips with his own limitations.

"Look, I know how this has to bother you."

"Of course it does," he snapped, slumping back in his chair. "It starts me thinking I'm getting past my time. And that, above all, really bothers the shit out of me."

chapter

TWENTY-
EIGHT

Oddly enough, Louie called me out of the blue. I was startled. "I need to talk to you." I could tell from the background noise he was calling from a pay phone.

I wasn't sure I wanted to talk to him. "What's it about?"

"I need your professional opinion about something. Don't worry. I won't take much of your time."

I knew I was in a predicament. If I turned him down, I would further arouse his suspicions, and that would only generate additional animosity and feelings of betrayal that I believed were percolating just below his surface. He had always seen himself as a kindred spirit and an influential figure in my life. Now we hardly spoke to each other. Oddly, I missed his friendship in ways with which I had yet to come to terms.

I realized my turning him down might make him think I was afraid of him. That would only embolden him or give him the idea he could extort me for information. But if I accepted his invitation, I faced prospect of being trapped and kidnapped, or killed and fitted for one of Louie's body bags and a fifty-pound bag of cement. With that a very real possibility, I realized I had better tell Noah about Louis' call.

"Tell you what then," I said to Louie. "Let me buy you lunch and we can talk it out over a sandwich or something. What do you say?"

That sounded good to him. "Lunch, really? Where?"

"How about the deli up at the Glen Centre?"

Ten minutes later I called Noah from a pay phone and told him about Louie's call. I knew that Noah used a state-of-the-art scrambler for his calls, so even at my house it was only my side of the call that could be understood. From the time they first found my house bugged I remained concerned that Louie's friends had a tap on my line. It was doubtful since Noah swept my house of everything but his own probable bugs a couple of times a week.

Just the same, I took the precaution of calling Noah from the Seven-Eleven. I think throughout its brief modern history the pay phones at Seven-Elevens have collectively hosted more calls involving intrigue, drug deals, and assorted illicit business than any other public phones on Earth.

"What did you tell him?" Noah asked me.

"I told him I would buy him lunch."

"And I told you I wanted you to stay away from him. It's dangerous now. And you know damn well he could go off without warning."

"I'm not going to act like I'm afraid of him. That's an invitation for him to try and work me."

"Make up some excuse. He'll probably forget about it in a couple of days."

"No. He'll find it offensive that I rejected him, and he'll start calling me for spite. Or he'll get really paranoid, and then I'll have a major problem on my hands. Whatever goes on in that fucking head of his is anyone's guess."

"Maybe you're right," Noah acknowledged reluctantly.

"Are you backing me up, or what? Or do I have to kill him just to be on the safe side?"

"I see," said Noah, his superior tone so rich in its condescension.

"You see what?"

"Since Yomiya you have acquired taste for it."

This was not so much an accusation as one of Noah's feelers. He was referring to the Red Brigade member I had shot.

"Yomiya was in self-defense." As the words left my mouth I knew it was stupid to argue. I was just playing into his hands.

"Well don't you go shooting old Louie. Not just yet."

"Then back me up."

The day I had lunch, Noah arranged for two federal agents to sit on the patio just a couple tables away from Louie and I. Although I didn't know the agents by name, I had recognized their faces from previous operations. They were a comfort to have around. I figured they were equipped to monitor any conversation electronically as well as with their own ears. Noah would definitely want a record of my little talk with Louie.

I arrived a few minutes early, allowing the agents time to position themselves at just the right table. Louie came a few minutes after our scheduled time. He was all smiles and walking slow, looking a little goofy as he approached the table. He was holding his arm stiff at his side, the way people do at the early onset of Parkinson 's Disease.

We sat down at a patio table and ordered sandwiches. Louie reminisced about the corn rye bread he used to eat as a little kid back in suburban New York, and I listened as if I cared.

"So what is it you wanted to ask me?" I asked, after swallowing a mouthful of sandwich.

Louie didn't bother waiting until he had swallowed. He tried to talk with a mouth full of food, and I was forced to bare witness to the destruction teeth can cause to pastrami, coleslaw and rye bread. I watched bits of Russian dressing dribble onto Louie's beard—a nice pink accent dabbed against the ashy hair. The humor was not lost on me that the tape recordings would memorialize a session of mastication and garbled words.

"Louis, please," I said. "Chew your food first. I'll wait."

"Oh, yeah," he apologized. "It's a bad habit. I came from the kind of house where everyone was in a hurry."

I nodded. Maybe that's why he shot his father. For talking with his mouth full. In any case, I believed Noah would appreciate my correcting Louie's table manners, so that our recorded conversation would at least be audible when logged for review.

"I was thinking about my life," Louie began again, having put down his sandwich. "I thought it has been a pretty interesting life, considering. I made mistakes, and all, but who hasn't, right?"

"We all make mistakes."

I knew he was leading up to something, but I wasn't sure what. I thought for a moment that he actually might want to confide in me about his working as a Chinese mole. I wondered how I would react if in between munches on his soggy French fries he launched into a confessional monologue. Then I wondered if in his on clumsy way he was preparing to threaten me without making it appear like a threat.

"I was thinking of writing a book about myself," he said, finally ending all my speculation. "You know something like a personal memoir. That's what you are doing with Noah, isn't it?"

"Yeah. Sort of. War stories."

"I was hoping you could work with me, too, and help me write it."

"I don't know. What's it about? Life as a dentist?"

He scoffed at me as if I were a fool. "You know there's more to my story than just being a dentist."

"Like what? Writing a book is harder than it seems. I would need to understand your entire story. What's in your story that would make it so exceptional?"

Louie shuffled nervously and played with his fries on the plate. "My work, for one thing."

"Dentistry?"

"No! Not that! "

"Louis, just what is it we're talking about?"

He stared hard at me, searching, and he found the blank stare of innocence staring right back in his face. Even Noah acknowledged I could be very convincing as an actor when I wanted. Noah regarded such natural skills of deception as invaluable assets that should be perfected over time and with the proper training. He assured me, with a little training, I could probably beat any polygraph test.

"Louis, you want me to help you write a book, and you won't tell me what the book is about. That's a little crazy, isn't it?"

"You know I could kill you for what you did," he suddenly snapped. He was speaking in a different voice; a different persona had suddenly stepped up to the plate. "It wouldn't be the first time, you know."

I knew sitting in his car somewhere, picking this up from the remote microphone the two nearby federal agents had aimed in our direction; Noah Brown was on the edge of his seat in anticipation.

"Louis, you know I care for you. I always have, and you know it. But let me say this...anything you put in your hands you'll be eating. So if you reach for anything, it would be wise to keep that in mind."

He stared hard at me for a good fifteen seconds, his gray eyes flashing as he contemplated his next move. I sensed he had it all rehearsed, everything he wanted to say to me, but now the script was blown.

"One gesture from me, and once you leave this table you'll never be seen again."

My impulse was to stick a fork through his eye, but Noah's lectures over time had taught me a greater restraint. Instead of a nasty retort I kept silent and waited for Louis to speak again.

"You were over my house. You saw that woman. You've been talking to Noah. You have to know more than you're letting on."

"What woman are you talking about?" I asked, cutting him off. "There have been quite a few women over your house. Some of them were cuter than others. Some of them were skanks, I've got to tell you. Dogs."

He laughed, partly frustrated and partly amused. The laughter was short and hard to come by, as if he was buying it at a premium price.

"I meant the Chinese woman," he said finally.

I knew for sure, Noah was practically chewing on the steering wheel.

"When was that?"

"The night of my nephew's party."

I pretended to think about it. I was a study in reflection. "Oh, her. What was that about, anyway?"

He stared hard at me again, assessing. "You saw."

I shook my head. "I have no fucking idea what you're even talking about."

I watched his face grow harsh with disappointment. My intuition had been correct. This was a set up, and Louie was on a fishing expedition. He was ready to sidle right up to the border of a confessional in order to bait the hook. Someone had put Louie up to this, I was sure.

I glanced around and caught sight of two pairs of hard looking techie types, wearing mean expressions. One pair was standing to my left, not twenty yards away, and the other pair was milling about the parking lot exit. One thing I had noticed about these kinds of guys, when they were angry, they had difficulty concealing their contempt for you. Wise guys and other tough guys would usually look at you with that dull, blank impassive stare. But these guys, no matter how hard they tried to hide it, couldn't conceal the loathing in their eyes. They looked like they must have looked as little kids when the bullies dumped their books or gave them wedgies. Then they took it, probably. But now they had guns for payback.

I knew the next few words that came out of my mouth would determine how things came down. If I said something wrong, Louie would signal the two pairs of heavies, and they would move in on me. Only then would they discover the FBI, or whatever agency my protectors were actually part of.

The surprise encounter could result in a very bloody shoot-out, and a number of spoiled and pretty, if not relatively innocent people, could be caught in the crossfire. The Glen Centre was crowded enough with routine activity, with those having lunch or running their errands. Any violent altercation could easily escalate into a gut wrenching tragedy. All that plastic surgery would go to waste. The ground littered with perfect noses. I didn't want that on my conscience. And besides, that would make headlines. Noah didn't want any headlines.

"You understand the meaning of loyalty?" Louie ventured.

"Of course I do."

Talk about a leading question. Coming from him, a question like that was so rife with irony and hypocrisy I didn't wish to dwell on it for fear I would break into laughter. Louie had tried to use me, and he had betrayed his country. Now he was worried that his seemingly minor transgressions, such as treason and murder, had turned me against him. For the briefest moment I almost hoped he would give his signal. An instant later my better senses again took hold of me.

"Louis, let me put it to you this way. Fate put us here at this table, but how we choose to leave it is a matter of our own volition. We share too much history to try to wrestle over conditions neither one of us could hope to control. So, until you are ready to write your book, let's just leave it go at that. You go your way, and I'll go mine."

I knew Louie always loved it when I used big words and spoke philosophically. To Louie, that made him feel included in some larger plan. He craved that inclusion. That's probably why he chose the wrong road to begin with. For a man who had been rejected most of his life, he craved people who would see him as their peer. He liked the feeling so much that he sold it with conviction to the many losers and misfits he picked up at the gun shows and the soirees. Christ, he tried to sell it to me.

Abruptly, Louie's psycho jukebox switched to another tune, and he became the avuncular, loving guy that I had first met in his dentist's office.

"Yeah," he said. His voice was deep and guttural, acknowledging from deep down or wherever he found his ephemeral sense of decency, a noble truth to my words. "Nothing else would make any sense."

I nodded. We finished lunch and left in peace. Louie was so filled with sentiment he insisted on hugging me in the middle of the parking lot. I hugged him back, feeling the .45 he had tucked in his shoulder holster. Shoulder holsters were easier to draw from in a seated position. Louie had come prepared. I ignored it, and to my surprise I found myself kissing him on the cheek. It was a reflex, without reason.

"You take care," I said.

"You, too."

All sentiment aside, I never turned my back on him. In case he had a sudden change of mood. I watched him climb in his car and drive away. I was relieved that we had both decided to give peace a chance.

chapter

TWENTY-NINE

In the middle of the night I heard an authoritative knock on the door and found Noah standing in my doorway. He was that kid again, that gung-ho Johnny G-Man that had first entered government services in the early forties. I watched him rubbing his hands together, a manifestation of the enthusiasm percolating inside him.

"You scared the hell out of me."

"Feel like taking a trip?" he asked, like he was restless and in need of spring break in Florida.

"I'll need coffee," I said.

"We'll pick some up on the way."

"So what's this about?" I asked, hoping this expedition was worth rising early and drinking bad coffee.

A few moments passed while Noah organized his thoughts, deciding how much to tell me.

"We spotted a possible satellite station. It is an illegal building on public land, and there was smoke coming out of the chimney. Infrared photography reveals a heat source all through the night. There is a Jeep parked outside. We tried to get the plate number, but it is backed so tightly against the wall, it's impossible to get the reading. And we think that's deliberate."

"So someone with sophisticated technological knowledge is living in a rustic cabin."

Noah agreed. "We're meeting a team up there. We're posing as Forest Rangers, poking around. It's our aim to present ourselves as a nuisance, but not appear threatening. You'll be one of those environmental nuts the government employs every once in awhile. A real tree hugger," he smiled.

By the middle of the afternoon I was climbing into one of a pair of Jeeps belonging to the United States Forest Service. In the first Jeep, the men were heavily armed with automatic weapons. They were designated to standby and respond in case of trouble. In our group, Noah and some of the others wore only side arms, if anything. From what I could tell the only genuine Forest Ranger was this good natured, but ham fisted giant of a senior supervisor, who was just a few months from retirement. I was sure in my absence Noah had sworn the man to an oath of secrecy.

Thirty mile per hour gusts of wind and intermittent but heavy showers ripped at the Jeeps, making the steep and winding, and very rutted, double cow path a difficult road to travel. If the Jeeps weren't bouncing, they were skidding in the mud. As we climbed further into the mountains, the temperature dropped into the low thirties and the rains turned into icy sleet. At last we came upon a sign that read "private road."

"That's bullshit," said the Forest Ranger.

"I have the feeling we've come to the right place," Noah mentioned as we bounced around inside the Jeep.

The suspicious cabin was hidden among the pines and nestled in a small clearing near the crest of the mountain. It was set just off a fire road that had been constructed on a good rock foundation, so there was little chance of it sliding away during winter storms. As we approached, we spotted the satellite dishes and the antennas bristling from their concrete platforms.

The Jeep was still parked against the wall, the license plate absent from its front bumper. A Ford Bronco was parked beside it. There were a plethora of oil drums alongside and in the back of the cabin. Their purpose was to collect the rainwater.

The building itself was larger than I had imagined, and it was constructed of cinderblock and poured concrete, the materials one rarely finds in a mountain cabin hideaway. The cabin windows were placed high up in strategic positions—no peeking inside. Prodigious solar panels covered the roof. We hadn't parked yet and already I could feel the apprehension doing a tap dance on my nervous system. I was reminded of the hundred thousand movies where the hapless teenagers venture up to a strange and foreboding house and are subsequently killed and eaten by its psychotic inbreds. I felt for a moment how Hansel and Gretel would have felt at the Gingerbread House, if only they knew better. And at the same time, had I the chance to choose again, I wouldn't have missed this for the world.

The real Forest Ranger rapped hard on the door.

"Hello inside," he called, rapping again with his big, meaty knuckles.

We heard stirring, then mumbling, and finally a voice that called out, "Just a minute."

One guy answered the door. He was tall and wide, muscular and yet a little pudgy from sitting around too much. His short blonde hair looked like he cut it with a clipper, and his faced boasted two day's growth.

"Can I help you?" he asked suspiciously.

The Forest Ranger spoke up. "We've been checking cabins in the area. Apparently there have been some fires from the electrical storms, as well as power outages. We hadn't noticed your cabin before, and we thought we had better check it out and make sure you're okay."

"We're fine," answered the man, switching modes and trying to be almost light hearted about it. For a hard ass he first appeared to possess an easygoing temperament. No wonder they picked him to answer the door.

"Mind if we come in for a minute?" Noah asked, his Ranger's hat slipping comically down over his brow. "We've been driving around for awhile."

The blonde haired man knew he would only raise our suspicions if he denied us entry. Shrugging like it was no big deal; he stepped back from the door.

"C'mon in," he gestured.

Once inside, we found two other men sitting in the main room, a cramped living room with an adjacent kitchen. The swarthy one wore a beard and tried to look affable in his glasses and Buffalo patterned flannel shirt. The bald guy wore a pale gray sweater that matched the color of his beady pig's eyes. In truth this did have all the potential for a B horror movie. Given their preferences, these guys would have just as soon boiled and eaten us as given up the time of day.

The room had eight-foot ceilings, and I noticed the front door was backed with stainless steel plating. Thick steel bars served as locks on the windows and locks on the doors. In spite of the fact that the doors leading to the other rooms in the cabin were closed, I thought I heard at least one other person hiding out. He was probably lurking with weapon in hand—the back-up. My eyes caught sight of a coat rack. There were four coats on the rack. Three or four additional pegs were empty. That meant a few more could be out and about, or watching us from exterior cover. I glanced at Noah, and he was noting the curtained shelving where large quantities of canned and packaged food were stored. I noticed that a brand new Mitsubishi wide screen color television was standing across the room.

Despite all attempts to the contrary, the tension on both sides was so great no one could overcome the growing period of silence. I watched muscles tense and eyes exchange furtive glances. It was a matter of time before the silence would reach critical mass and then the shit would hit the fan.

I think the shock of reality had relieved everyone of his social skills. The guys in the satellite station realized they had finally been discovered. As for our side, I believed everyone expected this to be a satellite station, but no one predicted it would all seem so glaringly obvious.

"So," I opened, catching everyone by surprise. "Are you doing your best to maintain proper environmental standards?"

Everyone looked at me like I was crazy. Except for Noah, who nodded, affirmatively. "Environmental standards are critical," he volunteered.

"Like what?" The guy with the beard and glasses cocked his head to one side, presenting his question as if he were challenging me.

"Waste disposal, for one thing," I offered, getting into my character. I rolled my eyes at Noah, signaling that I would soon be out of wilderness issues, and he could chime in any time. "You should always be careful as to how you dispose of your waste."

The guy with the beard gestured toward a set of picks and shovels. "We bury our waste. You one of those tree huggers?" he smiled cruelly, while looking around for someone to approve of his joke.

"Naw. I just fine people who persist on violating the codes."

That knocked the smile from his face.

"You had to notice the solar panels up on the roof," the blond crew cut volunteered as a peace offering. "When we can, we use only solar energy."

"And your coal oil heater," I pointed out.

"It's better than wood fires," he argued.

I nodded, grudgingly. I thought it was pretty funny that, among all of these hard asses, I was the guy who had them afraid.

"How do you run your computers?" Noah interjected, before it became obvious I was almost out of gas. "They have to use a lot of juice."

"They draw some 560 watts. But we don't run them all that often. We do most of our work on a legal pad."

"And fire safety?" Noah asked, handing the man a printed sheet detailing the dangers of carbon monoxide poisoning. "You know what can happen, if your place isn't adequately ventilated. You can die from the fumes."

I noticed on the men thin, surreptitious smiles. They had overcome their fear of discovery and now believed we were merely bureaucratic idiots caught up in minutiae. I watched them relax, believing that with a few terse explanations we would be on our way.

"We have a spark arrestor in the ceiling, and the entire place is ventilated well beyond minimum standards," offered the balding one.

"And the walls are concrete?" I added, like it actually meant something to me.

"Ten inches," was the reply.

"Do one of you guys own the place, or do you own it collectively?" I heard the Forest Ranger ask. It was a critical question, one we had neglected.

The men shifted around in their chair, glancing at each other uncomfortably.

"Actually, none of us owns it," said the crew cut blonde. The real owner pays me to watch over things, and he doesn't mind if these guys come up and hang with me. We're business associates. We run a computer programming business to service the needs of smaller companies."

We all nodded, as if it made perfect sense. Just the same, everyone knew it was bullshit.

"We'll check back from time to time," said the Forest Ranger. "To make sure you guys are doing alright."

They nodded. "You do that."

It was after dark when we returned to the nearest Travel Lodge, where a number of rooms had been reserved. One group tagged the audiotapes that had been secretly recorded and developed the film from hidden cameras. Noah and the others coordinated the directions among the three antennas that were aimed at the Chinese Consulate and the Old Holy Church in San Francisco and points in between. They were scaling the frequency emanating from the antennas by using a ruler and a compass. Somehow the ruler measured frequency, and the compass indicated direction of the broadcast. I never did understand the process entirely. Noah had explained it had something to do with the four-thirds law, which related to how the radio frequency was measured a third further than the diameter of the earth. I didn't even want to pretend it really mattered to me. I sat quietly and watched the news on TV.

"If we work fast, we could hit them before they know it and catch them with their pants down," someone was saying.

He was a Beltway Cowboy. Even across the room his body language betrayed his sense of self-importance. He considered himself Noah's peer and passed a condescending glance over the older man, as if he was a relic, the remaining slide rule in a computerized world. "If we wait," continued the Cowboy, "we're giving them time to prepare."

Noah nodded, not buying the logic. "What do you think?" he asked, turning to me.

Some of the others bristled that Noah had solicited my opinion, which is probably why he did it in the first place. I'm sure he also wanted to see if I would play it smart or go for the glory, this being the first time I was involved in an operation of this magnitude. I looked around the room. A few souls were receptive and accommodating, the rest viewed me with a mix of open condescension or hidden contempt or even jealousy. Most agents wait a lifetime to work this kind of case, and here I was the sidekick to a legend.

"They saw you today. Maybe they went for the story, maybe they didn't. If they went for the story, then you were just a bunch of Forest Rangers doing their duty. If they didn't believe you, then the word is out, and they will be waiting for you.

"I would take the chance that they bought into the story, or at the very least they weren't convinced either way. They'll be vigilant for a few days, a week, and then they will settle in, and things will return to the dull routine. Meanwhile you'll have time to plan the assault and make sure you have an adequate force."

"There're only three of them inside," the Cowboy argued.

"Four at least," I corrected.

The Cowboy didn't like that at all. My pointing out the obstacles had reduced the probability of any serious bonding between him and me. He was staring hard at me, and I stared back impassively.

"Just what are you doing here, anyway?" he had the temerity to ask me.

"Fulfilling my destiny," I told him with a completely straight face.

There was a brief lull of uneasy silence, and then the others broke out laughing. The Cowboy didn't get the joke, really, but he knew that without a witty retort he was best leaving it alone.

Noah managed a subtle smile of approval. "Those walls are constructed of cinderblock and ten inches of solid, reinforced concrete," he said, getting us back to business. "The cabin door is backed by solid steel. It's an eight hour fire door. The windows and doors all have steel bars. There is a hidden ventilation system. And you can be sure they have plenty of weapons and ammo. The place is a virtual fortress.

"To assault that cabin, while sustaining the least amount of casualties and inflicting the least amount of damage to its structure we will need a dark and stormy night, as they say. Intense fog. Visibility on that mountain is fifteen hundred feet on a good day. I want it down to near zero visibility."

"It'll take days at least, before we can assemble an adequate number of agents," someone argued. "Most have been diverted to operations up in San Francisco. So what do you suggest?"

Noah took his time opening new pack of cigarettes. He pulled one out, offered the pack to the others and then lit up with obvious deliberation. All eyes were on him, and he enjoyed the attention.

"Let me cut to the chase here," emphasizing through his deliberation that he was without doubt the top dog in this company.

"We've already taken down three other satellite stations. We did one in Colorado, one in the mountains of upstate New York, and the one in Hawaii. Each time we timed it so it would look like a natural disaster. Trouble is, by the time the battle was over, not everything inside the stations had been left intact. We need one that is still intact so that we can replicate it totally."

Exhaling smoke through his mouth and nose, he looked around the room. "Do I make myself clear?"

Silence and then the kind of muttering that signals grudging assent.

"Remember. When we take this station, it is essential that any evidence of its very existence disappear. It is imperative that they never learn why it happened or how it happened. We must do our best to convince them it was an accident, a natural disaster, anything but what it is."

"But there's still the issue of how are we going to pull this off with a limited force?"

Noah smiled. "I'll make a couple of phone calls."

chapter

THIRTY

The following day Noah and I drove up to Fort Ord, near Monterey, California. This old Army Base was located on some of the nation's more scenic grounds and had on more than one occasion been marked for closure. But political leverage from the politicians representing the interests of the Great State of California had managed to keep it operational. Despite all valiant efforts, its final closure was only a matter of time. Meanwhile it was home to the Seventh Light Infantry, which that spring was neither overburdened nor otherwise preoccupied with any real war effort. It would be fair to say that the Seventh was bored and looking for something exciting to do.

An hour later our liaison, Colonel Whitley, had mustered more than one hundred men to a training area. A few were the Sergeant Rock types of childhood comic book fame, the kind of blood and guts veterans who would rather die than give up a secret or let the enemy retake a hill. The rest of the men were a mix of younger junior officers and enlisted men, fit enough as Noah had requested to run five miles or more with sixty pounds on their backs.

"Men," Colonel Whitley began, practically busting with pride. "I am calling on volunteers for an exacting mission. We must neutralize the enemy. This mission is a clandestine operation, and it will be performed on a need to know basis. Again, I stress to all of you that this mission can never be made public, and anyone who does so will suffer the most grievous consequences as allowed by martial and civilian law. To say nothing of getting my boot square up your ass."

There was no shortage of volunteers. In fact it took Noah longer to pick from a list of very capable candidates than it did to brief them on the mission itself. Noah explained in detail to Colonel Whitley the function of the operation.

"We must wait for the proper weather," Noah explained. "So you have time to train them for this specific operation."

"My men will be ready," Colonel Whitely assured us. "I will be leading this force," he noted with pride.

"We'll notify you and make all advance preparations then. Thank you, Colonel," said Noah, extending his hands, and the grateful Colonel shook hands all around.

We drove out of Monterey, and instead of heading south; we went north to San Francisco. Since Noah hadn't mentioned anything about a trip to San Francisco, I sensed there had been either a sudden change of plans, or this was the kind of secret operation Noah would not dare disclose beforehand.

"What's up?" I asked finally as we pulled up to the Fairmont Hotel on Nob Hill. "These are fancy digs and not the usual shit hole. The shock is almost too much."

"It is sometimes good to be seen and duly noted."

"Yeah. Maybe. But something is biting at you. You have the look of a man confronting his own mortality."

"You're reading my mind," he smiled. "See? We have a psychic connection."

"You're not going New Age on me, are you?"

"Well I did spend time on Project Blue Book. I had the desk then for the DIA. I saw a couple of things we couldn't explain."

"The spook believes in ghosts. Can I come along?"

"No, not this time. You read it right. I don't like the feel of tonight's little shindig. I'm afraid we'll get hurt."

Less than three hours later, I was sitting alone in our hotel room, watching television and sipping an Irish whiskey I had selected from the courtesy bar when I first heard the sirens. I knew intuitively it related to Noah and his hunting party. I went to the window and pulled back the drapes. A fire raged in the distance. Flames and smoke were reaching hundreds of feet into the sky.

I switched the television to a local channel and listened to a nervous reporter explain that, according to witnesses, a series of explosions had erupted from the Mayfield Building and then the building was engulfed by flames. The Mayfield Building was a three story commercial structure that was situated on a full square city block. An unknown number were dead, and at least twenty people had been hospitalized for injuries.

I tossed back the Irish and fetched another one from the courtesy bar. I needed details. I changed channels and it was the same basic information. The Mayfield Building had been home to more than one hundred shops and assorted small businesses. It was a notable San Francisco landmark...blah, blah...Well, not anymore.

Noah returned to the hotel room several hours later. He was exhausted and angry, covered with ash. He looked so crazed I'm sure he would have paced the floor throughout the night, had his withered legs allowed it.

"You want something to drink?" I asked, and he looked grateful. It was an excuse to slow down.

"Scotch is preferable. What have you been drinking?"

"Irish."

He nodded and accepted the scotch on the rocks I offered.

"Is that your work?" I asked. I gestured out the window as the fire continued to ravage the Mayfield Building.

"One of our guys got shot up pretty badly. I know we killed at least two of theirs."

"They were waiting for you?"

Noah shook his head, no. "This was their central head-quarters for illegal munitions manufacturing. From here they fed raw materials to what used to be their Phoenix and Albany operation. They had stepped up operations and were trying to duplicate equipment so they could re-establish their weapons and munitions manufacturing operations in other parts of the country."

"How long have you known about this?"

Noah gestured toward the courtesy bar. I could see he was almost too weary to stand. I filled his glass with fresh ice and then retrieved another small bottle of scotch for him. We waited in silence while I emptied the scotch into his glass.

"How long have we known?" he muttered, as if only now the events and tragedies of what had taken place were only coming clear to him. "We had been watching for couple of months, learning what we could about their distribution. We figured it was time to go inside."

I watched him toss back most of his scotch. He paused and lit a cigarette, finding solace in that first long drag.

"There was a team of eleven of us. The place was booby-trapped. We were maneuvering around the booby trap when one of the bad guys spotted us. Weapons were drawn and the shooting began. We were retreating when a stray shot hit something explosive, and the whole place blew. The two that were doing most of the shooting at us died in the initial blast. As for the rest, it was hard to tell. We just beat it the hell out of there.

"You know what else?" Noah offered as if it had just occurred to him. "The shipping insignias from all their different computer companies were printed and stored in that warehouse. That ties the computer companies into the illegal munitions plants. We would have discovered so much more, had not the building been lost. Dammit! This is quite a mess."

I gestured toward the window. "It's been all over the news."

Noah nodded in understanding. "I was just with the heads of the police and fire departments. We are reporting it as an illegal fireworks plant."

I stared incredulous. "And you expect people to go for that?"

He nodded. "They have believed more outrageous explanations than this one. I don't see why not." He threw me a look. "Unless somebody talks."

"I'm too busy drinking. What about you?"

He laughed. "Sorry. It's been a long night."

It was a long night, and I stayed up with him through most of it, drinking dry the courtesy bar and watching the building burn. Several days later, newspapers duly reported that the fire that had killed nine and wiped out over one hundred shops and businesses clustered in a square city block was caused by an illegal fireworks factory that had been fronted by a supposed storage company.

The city officials did their best to make the bullshit story seem plausible. The fire chief claimed they had found black powder and various fireworks assembly equipment. The owner of the building, of course, had no idea there was an illegal operation housed in building. A captain in the San Francisco Fire Department said that they were seeking warrants for the arrest of up to six individuals. An investigator from the Federal Bureau of Alcohol, Tobacco and Firearms wouldn't confirm or deny that any warrants were being sought. The Assistant U.S. Attorney denied that any warrants were being sought, and the searchers believed the bodies were so badly charred it they would be difficult to identify.

The fireworks story not only proved to hold water, but the whole operation and cover proved so successful that it was used again a couple of months later in Albuquerque, New Mexico. No one ever put the two stories together.

chapter

THIRTY-ONE

Two weeks later the weather bureau reported a heavy electrical storm was due to sweep in from off the Pacific Coast and bring high winds and heavy rains to the mountains south and east of San Francisco. It was the occasion the Feds had all been waiting for. Noah notified Colonel Whitley, and the volunteers from the Seventh Light Infantry started moving into their designated staging area. Two carloads of federal agents drove up to establish a command post. Noah and I drove up to the staging area in his Corvette that following morning. The predicted storm wasn't due for another couple of days, but there were things to be coordinated, supplies to be gathered, and some advance work that needed attending.

Several recluses who lived in the area were politely encouraged to leave for a week or so. Vacation spots were suggested, and each recluse was given enough cash to compensate him for the inconvenience. A pair of agents was assigned to visit a nearby college hospital and pick up a cadaver, as previously arranged. A surveillance plane, an unmanned drone was trucked in and concealed in a nearby garage.

"The volunteers from the Seventh are bivouacked in a warehouse," Noah explained. "People will get suspicious, if they catch sight of them. Even our guys could raise eyebrows, if we hang around too long. Everyone knows his assignment. The idea is to wait for the storm and then bring everything together."

"What about the dead wino? What's his assignment?"

"Don't kid yourself. That wino has a major role to play."

Most of your life the last thing you are hoping for is lousy weather. But the following night we actually welcomed the thick, foggy chiaroscuro brought on by the lightning and thunder. It was like watching the world through a somber white veil. And then winds came, followed by the rain. Both were light at first, but as the hours ticked on, and as we drove sans headlights up that narrow mountain fire trail, the winds threatened to blow one of the vehicles axle deep in mud.

As we climbed higher into the mountains, the fog grew thicker, and it was all the driver could do to keep us on the road. At last we came up about a good two miles from the satellite station. The drivers killed their engines, and the assault team and the communications personnel climbed out of their vehicles and started checking gear. Satisfied all was right, the communications group set up shop in their special truck, making sure that the wireless radios worn by the volunteers from the Seventh, as well as the federal agents, were fully operational.

"Look, no one has to die here," Noah admonished Colonel Whitley and the combat leader of the federal team. There are at least four and maybe seven of them inside. Let's play it smart, and we will all go home tonight."

The skies opened up, and the rain began to pour down on the men as they noiselessly checked out weapons and night vision apparatus, as well as explosives. When they were finished, each team moved out to its strategic position and waited for the command to begin the assault.

"We are ready for the drone," Noah called in over the radio. "You want to guess who the pilot is?" he challenged.

"You didn't? You really stuck the dead wino in there?"

Noah shrugged. "It has to look good. A lone pilot flying a private plane during a terrible storm is struck by lightning and crashes into a cabin that was constructed illegally on public land."

"So that's how this plays out."

"I hope so. We'll see, soon enough."

A few minutes later the sound of a smaller airplane engine could be heard in between thunderclaps. I looked up to try and find it among the clouds, but I never did catch sight of it until it was in the final stages of its dive. For that split second I caught its shadow as it plunged and crashed against the enemy vehicles parked alongside the satellite station.

"Shit!" Noah exclaimed as we watched the drone explode into flames. "Fucking wind shifted, and with all that extra weight inside…"

It didn't seem to matter much. Members of the assault team laid down heavy suppressive fire with automatic weapons while others rushed the satellite station from different directions. They were advancing steadily, moving from tree to tree.

The lights in the station went out and the men inside opened fire with automatic weapons.

"There must be motion sensors around the place," Noah realized. "They know in which direction to shoot."

Gunfire was echoing off other mountains and canyons, as tracer bullets pierced the heavy fog. Every animal in the wilderness had to be wondering—what the hell was going on? Two members of the assault team reached the walls of the satellite station and used an explosive bar to break through the steel reinforced window. Two more came up and heaved in a pair of concussion grenades. I observed from a distance the white flashes and heard the explosions that were designed to disorient the enemy. Two more concussion grenades were lobbed through the window as another team set charges on the steel reinforced door. The door blew, and men wearing night vision scopes rushed inside, firing their automatic weapons. It was over in seconds.

One soldier appeared in the doorway, waving his weapon. "All clear!" he shouted for all to hear. A cheer went up from some of the guys.

Seven men had attempted to defend the mountain satellite station, and the seven men had lost their lives. Not one team member was seriously injured. Later, the autopsies on the defenders would show that most of the men inside were no strangers to combat. Their body scars revealed previous gunshot wounds, severe knife cuts and other evidence of violent encounters. The autopsies also determined that at least two of the men were of a mix of German and Asian lineage. None of the men carried any identification, and there were no matches on any of the fingerprint samples.

It took most of the night to sort things out, since much of the station was booby-trapped.

"What do you think?" Noah asked, escorting me from the rear staging area to the cabin. "It went off just like we planned. And the dead wino gave his all for his country."

I glanced toward the doorway. The first of the defenders was being carried out in a body bag. Someone motioned to Noah, and he held out his arm so I could take it and help him negotiate the muddy trail that led up to the house. I waited outside, and he entered the station to take stock of the place. I studied the volunteers who were sitting around, reflecting on their assault. Everyone was happy with the results. Everyone was alive.

It wasn't long before I heard the rumble of heavy equipment. Dump trucks and flat trucks, carrying bulldozers were advancing up the hill. Behind them were several transports. When they drew near the entrance of the cabin, they jumped out of the transports and started toward the house. The bulldozers were rolled off the flatbeds and were readied for action. Noah stepped out to greet the new arrivals.

"We think we got all the booby traps, but be careful just the same. All the equipment is still intact, and I want to be sure it remains that way."

Along with the computer equipment, the wide screen television, and the basic stuff that was needed for living, the searchers turned up fourteen automatic weapons, including several automatic M-16's, half dozen shotguns and eleven nine-millimeter pistols. There were more than three thousand rounds of ammunition inside, and there was enough food to last for six months. The assault team also found second story tools, including lock picks and rubber gloves, codebooks, and six cyanide capsules.

The four-wheel Toyota was a stolen vehicle that had been registered in Colorado. It would be later discovered that its California license plates came from a wreck in a junkyard in Oakland, California, and the current stickers, showing the date and year, were stolen from another car. The interior of the satellite station was photographed in detail. They took inventory before loading the cabin's equipment.

"It is the same kind of equipment we found at the other satellite stations," Noah confided. "I would say this is very convincing evidence that all the stations are related. Even the building materials are similar, although this was the toughest nut to crack. But look at all this equipment. This was the mother lode."

"What do you do with this stuff?" I asked later on.

He thought about playing coy, but decided against it. He was in too good a mood. "It's all taken to a super secret building in Hawaii where we reassemble everything, according to the photographs. Once we finish we'll know how it works, and we will finally be able to communicate with the Chinese satellites. We'll be able to decode their messages, whether they are transmitting or receiving. Then the fun will really begin."

Before the operation was over, the bulldozers would raze the building, and the dump trucks would haul away every bit of building material, including the concrete foundation. The transports would carry off intact nearly two and a half tons of technological equipment. The only testimony to what had taken place was a sign that was posted. It read—"Removed by U.S. Forestry Service due to illegal structure. No records of permits have ever been filed."

chapter

THIRTY-TWO

In the days and weeks following the assault on the satellite station, Noah was busy traveling from Washington, D.C. to Hawaii, and from time to time he was making additional trips to Sandia Laboratories in Albuquerque and the laboratories in Los Alamos, New Mexico. In the brief time we shared together, Noah offered less information, and out of courtesy I refrained from asking him very much. I had a feeling that the entire investigation had reached a critical plateau, and that neither Noah Brown nor much of our national leadership had any true grip on the problem.

Three months had gone by when I received a call from Noah, inviting me to dinner. We met as usual at the Beverly

Glen Centre. But instead of the usual pizza that night, I was invited to more formal dining at Adriano's. It was where it had all started—our first meeting. That alone should have told me something was up, but I believed he wanted to discuss the ongoing news reports that were emanating now from every news outlet. Chinese espionage was now a common topic of discussion by media pundits and self-appointed experts. But being the end of the eighties, it was a time when the period of affluence was facing what some perceived as an economic downtown.

Few knew the worst of it, but nevertheless a general malaise was starting to build, and with it a willful lack of concern about anything that existed beyond the typical celebrity worship. Like most stories of forewarning that reached the media, former policy makers and a more current collection of windbags pitted their political ideology against the increasingly news numb consciousness of a confused and apathetic public.

"We are winding down our general operation," Noah confided that night over dinner. He was nervous and reluctant to admit that the investigation didn't have quite the pop he once had hoped for. "We are only concentrating on specific areas."

"Just what are you saying?"

"Like I told you before, too many people are afraid of making waves. The business interests believe we shouldn't risk derailing our greater long term financial involvement in China."

"It's probably a smart move in the long run. A smart move, even if they are arming themselves by stealing American weapons and technology."

I said it dryly, enough so that Noah wasn't sure if I was being serious or not.

"It's costing us billions of dollars and millions of jobs, to say nothing of our military advantage. They're building their military forces, and creating an offensive structure."

"But, as you said, no one is prepared to do all that much about it."

He shook his head and picked up his wine glass, pretending to examine it as he spoke to me. "It's not my choice," he sighed. "But you know the deal. The conglomerates pressure the lobbyists and the lobbyists pressure the politicians. The conglomerates also pressure the State Department, and especially their friends in the Executive Branch. They pass it down to us. We eat shit, and the world keeps spinning 'round."

"So...What will you do?"

He shrugged. "I might call it a day."

"You mean, live an ordinary life?"

"Nothing ordinary about it. I have my science projects. I'd love to write several books. And that takes time. Maybe it's time I made the change."

I sat back and nodded. "However this ends, it's been a valuable education up until now. I'm grateful you treated me to front row seats."

I watched him deliberate. He slid a cigarette out of its pack and then replaced it. Having reconsidered, he removed the cigarette, finally, and lit it up. I watched in silence as he blew out the smoke. The woman sitting at the adjacent table made little coughing noises to indicate the smoke was annoying her. Noah didn't seem to notice, and if he did, he certainly didn't care.

"There is a way for you to stay in the game," he whispered, leaning forward so to avoid eavesdroppers. His voice was projecting the kind of hope terminal patients seek in their last days of existence.

I stared and waited. I couldn't wait to hear this one.

"There is someone in San Diego. We need information he keeps in a vault in his house. And after it has been relieved from his person, we don't want him telling anyone it is missing."

"You want him dead?" I asked, coming to the point.

I watched him nod. "We figured that would be the best solution."

"Why not just burglarize his place?"

"He has to disappear, for reasons I can't go into. I can give you five thousand up front, and you can keep anything you find there."

"Like what?"

"Computers. Electronics. Whatever you find."

I let several awkward moments lapse into an uncomfortable silence. I realized then that this was an unavoidable direction that was always an inherent part of our association. I knew he liked me, but Noah couldn't help himself. Maybe he believed he had to get something else out of it, other than a sudden and amicable parting. Perhaps he needed to wring that extra mile from my tank of gasoline. Or, for his own deep-rooted satisfaction, he wasn't finished until he had turned me into...him.

"I sense a serious lapse in our mutual understanding here."

"What's the problem? You took care of Yomiya."

"So this is the end game? You want to convert me to a hired killer. Pimp me out. I guess in one perverse way it's a form of recycling."

"This man is a threat to the American public."

"So is fast food. If you really understood me, you would have known what the answer would be."

He shrugged and showed me his nice guy smile. "I can't help it. I guess it's the nature of the beast."

I nodded. "That's why some beasts go extinct before others."

Noah stared hard at me. For the first time since I knew him, he looked genuinely hurt. My words, my anger had finally pierced that skin.

"I'm sorry I asked the question," he whispered in a voice that was barely audible.

I nodded and left it alone.

chapter

THIRTY-THREE

Although I seldom traveled with Noah anymore, we still met for lunch or spent many nights sitting and talking out different situations. He was angry and prone to the occasional rant. He would then regain himself and feign acceptance, until the frustration built up inside like so much steam, and then the whistle had to blow.

"I tell them what I think," he lamented. "But no one seems to care."

"You do. You still care."

"What's that worth to anyone?"

"It's who you are. So it's a matter of what it's worth to you."

"It's worth a pension," he allowed in resignation. He was probing his forefinger around his ear and examining the findings.

"I told you up front you would never find the main guy who ran the Chinese networks. Maybe there is no main guy. Or maybe it really is that old geezer you pointed out to me. I doubt it, myself."

He eyed me, nodding his head. "Just once, I'd like a Hollywood ending."

I stared and said nothing. He was fully aware of what my silence conveyed. He and I had come a long way. We had started on a mountain of misunderstanding. Now, like an old couple, fundamental gestures substituted for lengthy explanations and simple actions signified our love and concern for each other. Besides, Noah wasn't looking well, and despite his initial denials about his health, I realized he was beginning to deteriorate. This alone made the troubles in the world seem increasingly less significant.

"Pay attention to the news," he whispered to me not long after. "Something's coming that will show Americans what China is really all about. It took twenty years of assets to make this deal happen. It will leave a lasting impression."

The dramatic scenario that Noah predicted turned out to be the demonstrations in Tiananmen Square. Nothing did more to turn American public opinion than watching Chinese students and dissidents, who for six weeks gathered in the thousands and demanded their human rights. Nothing did more to turn American stomachs than to see these embattled people being overrun by Chinese tanks and slaughtered by ignorant factions of the Chinese Army that were brought in from the rural provinces for just this occasion.

The American public was sickened and demanded reconsideration of our policy with China. For once the American government didn't vacillate. Contracts for further satellite launches were rescinded until further notice, as were joint military initiatives, technology exchanges and consideration of Chinese admission to the World Trade Council.

However, contrary to what Noah had predicted, Tiananmen Square failed to leave a lasting impression. Cheap electronics, and cheaper clothes from Big Box stores—they leave a lasting impression. Three years after Tiananmen Square, perceptions turned around and China was again awarded special treatment. In the years to follow, the American forces advocating containment of China would do battle with the forces that encouraged peaceful engagement. The two sides would often come to a stalemate, and American policy toward China would reflect the ambiguities that had existed from the time President Richard Nixon first went to hang out with Mao Tse Tung.

For Noah Brown, it didn't matter anymore. "I've had enough," he confided bitterly in the early part of 1993. "I'm moving out of here to somewhere where I can just sit and do research and study my science. Members of my family all lived to a ripe old age, and I figure I have a good twenty, thirty years to tinker around in my laboratory."

Noah would never have his thirty remaining years. He was soon diagnosed as seriously ill. Depending on which doctor was speculating, he had either pancreatic cancer that they couldn't fully detect, or he was suffering from years of exposure to electromagnetic and atomic radiation. On the bottom line, his body was falling apart one vital organ at a time.

I visited him often. He wasn't eating much, so he was losing weight and assuming the skeletal contours evident in someone dying. His rapidly thinning hair was shorn to a crew cut, and he talked more softly and he walked with ever increasing difficulty. Where his pride once forbade him to ask for assistance, he now eagerly offered his arm, and I would help him to stand or sit or merely walk across the room.

He sold his house of thirty odd years and moved to an area in Central California that most resembled the Golden State of his youth. It was still a small village, vintage forties and fifties California, the kind of pastoral simplicity that was rapidly disappearing along with the myth and at least part of the California dream. The area surrounding his new residence resembled the colorful vintage stickers on the orange crates of an earlier and far more innocent era. Acres of orange and avocado trees surrounded his mountain top house and dominated much of the landscape. He was genuinely happy there, and I was grateful since, clearly, he had so little time.

"Do you think I did the right thing with my life?" he asked one afternoon. I had come to visit and to have lunch. Noah lacked the appetite for his sandwich and was content to lie in the chaise and let the sun beat on his face.

"Or do you think I wasted it, fighting for a lot of nonsense? I know if I hadn't gotten into all this, I would have been a different man."

"You were true to your convictions. That's all anyone can ask for."

"I know. But sometimes I think my best efforts went for nothing. I feel I was caught between being a builder and a destroyer. At the end of the day I was always the scientist."

"You know as well as I do. You live with your memories. Some of those memories are painful regrets."

"And you? What happens now?"

"I can never go back the way I came. That path is far behind me now. Let's face it; I was on the wrong path, acting out
with the wrong set of characters and wasting my time. You...this
experience, it brought me around to someplace else. Where exactly? I don't know. What I do know is that you put me through
a lot of changes."

"So, do I have your gratitude? Or did I end up leaving you
stranded?"

"A little of both, I guess. "What the hell? Like my grandmother used to say, it's a ride."

He smiled, faintly. For that moment he was looking
younger and healthier than he had in awhile. "Well, we gave it
our best. It just wasn't good enough."

"Maybe that's what it's all about," I went on. "We go
through those changes and the world stays the same. Or it moves
on, regardless of what we do or what we believe. If we're lucky,
we'll catch God in a good mood. And he'll let us come to terms
with our demons. Afterward, instead of growing bitter, we may
look for some way to make a contribution to the world. Nothing
major. Just something that makes people laugh or feel better
about themselves. Because one thing is for sure, hindsight and
history are cruel fucking teachers."

"You're glad I didn't hurt Louie? I know that would have
bothered you."

I nodded. "It would have been tough to live with. There's
just that something about Louie, no matter how crazy he is. Besides, you always had a soft spot for him. I knew it would be
difficult for you to do Louie."

Noah shrugged and in a rare moment of candor asked
himself more than I the obvious question. "What good what it

do? I guess that was my reasoning. He would have been judged insane and committed to an asylum."

"You didn't want him locked away. And you didn't want to kill him. You must be getting soft in your old age."

In a rare display of affection, Noah put his hand on my shoulder. He was smiling, and I sensed it was with the kind of pride he wasn't used to.

"You were always meant to be more than you settled for. It's time you caught up to your potential."

I nodded, thinking about what he said.

"Another thing," he said, turning somber. "I don't want you coming around anymore. I mean it. You hear?"

I could feel my face change expression. "So this is it?"

"I'm dying. You know that, and so do I. Although it's hard for me to believe. Shit."

I understood. He was a proud man and didn't want me to witness his final state of decay.

He died after falling into a coma. When Noah had first taken ill, I learned that Laura, his alleged housekeeper, was in reality Noah's wife of many years. He was never a widower. His four children were hers. It was his way of protecting her, of preventing people from going through her to get to him.

"He came out of his coma for just a few minutes," Laura told me. "That last thing he said was, 'Get me my pants. I want to go home.'"

There was very small funeral service. Like other men who lived in the shadows, no dignitaries attended; there was no long procession of vehicles from the church to the cemetery. His community in science and government would assimilate his memory, and secretly they would honor and entomb him in their hearts and minds. Noah was cremated, and a tree was planted over his ashes.

I learned from Noah's family that his computers had been wiped clean of everything but video games and basic programs. In a prescient moment he may have erased them himself, so he could take all his secrets to the grave with him. Or someone else could have erased them after his death. I never did find out. There was no way to do so. The deleted information, like so many other things, would be lost to the ages.

Louis Dubin died of natural causes about seven years after Noah. It was fitting they passed on, before the new century could really get underway. Truly, they were of another era and that era had given way to the new world of globalization and the incumbent crises and tribulations facing this era.

However, Chinese espionage did not end with the century. In the 1990's the news media was rife with news stories about Chinese spying practices and what it cost the American economy. To this day headlines appear with regular frequency where Americans and Chinese Nationals are arrested for passing military and technological secrets. Chinese relations with the United States have become interchangeably cause for concern or reasons for engaging, depending upon perspective. The ultimate resolution will most likely be left to future generations. As one of the few points of irony, the two nations are so interdependent, they seem bound now by a mutual destiny. Such is life.

As for life on a more personal level, its mystical elements of fate and circumstance can impose their will against even the more determined souls. Hopefully, we are left as improved characters with a redefined sense of direction. Be it me or some of the others. It was time to move on.

Made in the USA